THE
HITCHHIKERS

6

Other Scholastic titles
you will enjoy:

Hostilities
Caroline Macdonald

Prom Date
Diane Hoh

Bonemeal: Seven More Tales of Terror
Edited by A. Finnis

Cat-Dogs and Other Tales of Horror
Edited by A. Finnis

Thirteen
Edited by Tonya Pines

point

THE HITCHHIKERS

Stories from Joy Cowley

SCHOLASTIC INC.
New York Toronto London Auckland Sydney

ISBN 0-590-73904-2

12 11 10 9 8 7 6 5 4 3 2 1   7 8 9/9 0 1 2/0

Printed in the U.S.A.   01

First Scholastic printing, August 1997

For Terry,
who is close to the sea
and all living things.
With love and gratitude,
Joy

The original publisher gratefully
acknowledges the assistance of the
Literature Programme of the QEII Arts
Council in the publication of this book.

Contents

Contents

Acknowledgements

The poem "The Story Teller" (from *The Hitchhikers*) is reprinted by permission of Learning Media, Ministry of Education, Wellington.

Most of the stories in this collection have been broadcast by the "Ears" programme of Radio New Zealand.

THE HITCHHIKERS

Stories from Joy Cowley

Introduction

Since the beginnings of communication, people have used fantasy to express truths which could not be contained in a factual account. Many of these early stories gave explanations for unaccountable phenomena: why this mountain is so high or why that bird cries at night. Some of the more powerful stories lasted for generations and eventually became legends and some, which gave meaning to people's existence and were considered sacred, were enshrined as myth.

This collection of stories shows the influence of countless legends, myths, folk tales and fairy tales. As a child I devoured such fantasy stories with large appetite. I went through all of Andrew Lang's collections several times, I cried over Oscar Wilde's fairy tales, shuddered with Hans Christian

Andersen and the brothers Grimm, read and reread legends from Scandinavia, Russia, Greece, Ireland, North America and Aotearoa.

These stories were always glimpses into other times, other cultures, while all round me there was the empty space of 20th century Aotearoa-New Zealand, my time and my country. Like the rest of Aotearoa-New Zealanders, I came under the spell of the land and sea and heard their voices whispering of the enchantment which lay behind everyday things. But the only stories I had were the old, old legends of pre-Pakeha days. Where were the stories of my generation?

They were all there, waiting to be recorded, and now, many writers are doing just that. Once I began "listening" with my eyes, these tales came thick and fast and directly out of my environment. Some stories come directly from experience. "Cottage by the Sea" wrote itself after I visited a place which I had seen many times in my dreams. Other tales have been inspired by geographic features: the Moeraki boulders in "The Hitchhikers," a paddock of ripe wheat in the wind of "The Sea of Peace," and Mount Stokes in the Marlborough Sounds models for my "Totara Hill." Still others have begun with an encounter with some creature; a pet rooster "Rangi Tama-hehe," and a giant eel "Tarama."

Whatever the trigger for the story, all these tales belong to the South Pacific and to a country that is as much a part of me as is my own bone and blood.

The Sea of Peace

Brian swam to the opposite bank and back again. Under the willows the river was black and cold against his sunburnt skin. He couldn't touch the bottom. Further away, the water came out from its green cover and spread over stones, shallow and noisy, full of sunlight, but this was the best swimming hole.

A dozen laps and his arms pimpled with the cold. He climbed out, tied his towel round his waist and carried his clothes up the slope to the cowyard where he dressed in the sun. The concrete was so hot that his wet footprints shrank and dried in seconds. Before he'd buttoned his shirt, he was sweating again.

His parents were in town for the day. They'd been so apologetic and insistent about leaving him behind, that he guessed they were planning to buy him a birthday present. He would be eighteen in two days time. They'd probably be going from one shop to another, arguing in their slow, serious way, looking for something that was at once birthday present, consolation prize and bribe, a gift designed to solve all problems. Actually, he had only two problems but they were big enough to fill his life. He'd failed Bursary and he couldn't get a job.

His father kept telling him how lucky he was. "You've always got a job here on the farm. There are thousands like you don't have it so good."

Brian tied his boots. Maybe after the wheat harvest he'd head for Christchurch and chance his luck with some of those thousands on the dole. At least there were thousands, not just one on his own in the middle of nowhere.

The wind was getting up, hot and dry, made visible with dust and bits of straw. He stood up and looked towards the wheat fields that were rippling like a full tide. With the wind, and the heat haze shimmering above the surface, the entire crop looked so liquid he could imagine himself diving in and swimming in a sea the colour of pale honey.

Then he blinked away the daydream. Someone was out there. In the nearest wheat paddock. Someone was walking in it, leaving a dark path of trampled stalks.

An angry voice came up inside him, sounding like his father. He thought the words, What the hell do you think you're doing? but he didn't say them.

It was a woman walking in the wheat. She was dressed in wheat colour and she had long, dark hair. She seemed to be coming towards him.

He leaned against the cowyard railing and watched her climb through the fences. She was young. From the way she was dressed — long skirt, a shawl round her shoulders — he guessed she'd come from the commune six kilometres the other side of the river. He waited, squinting against the sun, and as she came closer, he realised she was pretty. Man, she was really beautiful. His heart moved sideways in his chest and for a second he felt a strange emptiness there. She was just about the loveliest girl he'd ever seen and he knew her. Yes. No, he didn't. He tried to think. He was confused. Something in him knew, even from this distance, that her eyes were light grey and the bridge of her nose, freckled. The rest of him had never seen her before.

She came up the hill to the cowshed, looking up at him and laughing. Certainly she knew who he was, for now she was running and holding her hands out to him.

"Freddy!" she called. "Freddy, I've come!"

He felt a keen disappointment. No, he didn't know her, and she had mistaken him for someone else.

"Freddy! My dearest Freddy!"

Her voice was young and shaped by some foreign accent. She'd be about sixteen, he thought. But the strange thing was, she was wet, drenched from head to foot as though she'd been in a thunderstorm. He knew then that she must have come from the commune. She must have crossed the river at a deep hole and fallen in.

"Freddy?" She stopped, a few paces from the railings. Her smile quivered and she lowered her arms.

"Sorry, I'm Brian." He was sorry, too. At that moment he would have given anything to be Freddy.

"Freddy Dysart! It's me, your Agnes." Her eyes were the palest grey, full of light, and now showing anxiety. Her dark hair clung to her forehead and dripped over her shoulders. The dress, with its long skirt, was wrapped tight and wet against her body.

She answered his gaze by drawing her shawl about her and hugging it. "Freddy, are you cross with waiting? I came as fast as I could but the way was long." Her voice trailed off. "So very long," she whispered.

"My name isn't Freddy. It's Brian. Brian McPhee. Are you staying at the commune?"

She didn't answer but held the shawl against her and shivered. "They say Pacific means sea of peace but it were no way peaceful with one storm after another and the drinking water bad. I couldn't come quicker, Freddy. I got lost."

He saw that her eyes had an unfocussed look and he thought, lost is right. She's on something. He said, "You shouldn't have tried to cross the river. There's a bridge further up. Didn't they tell you?"

She shook her head. In spite of the sun's baking heat, her shivering had increased.

He reached out to touch her arm and immediately drew back his hand. "You're freezing!"

"It's the fever, Freddy," she said through chattering teeth.

Well, at least she was responding to him. He gave her his towel. "Here, rub your hair with that. I'll go up to the house and get you some dry clothes. What's your name? Agnes? Wait here."

Her eyes became big with alarm. "Don't go! Don't leave me! Freddy, I want you to take me home."

"I'm Brian. Get it? Bri-an. I'll take you home when you're dry."

"No, Freddy!" She held her arms out to him.

"I'll be back," he said.

As he went up the path, he thought he should have taken her back to the house to get changed. He didn't know why he hadn't, except that it was his parents' house and they were dead against drugs.

He was, too, he'd discovered. It made him really angry the way people rubbished their brains with dope, especially when they were as beautiful as she was.

He got a dress from his mother's wardrobe, some underthings and a woollen cardigan which he stuffed into a supermarket bag. Even now, there persisted a feeling that he knew the girl. It was as though they'd been brought up together when they were little kids, that kind of feeling. But her accent was strange and he'd never known anyone called Agnes. He was sure of that.

When he went back to the yards, he called several times to let her know he was coming. There was no answer. He thought maybe she was undressed and hiding round the side of the milking shed. He called again. The towel was over the rail where she'd been standing and her shawl was lying on the ground. The girl had vanished. He wandered round the sheds and through the house paddock, calling her name. He looked in the orchard. He got out the binoculars and searched hectares of waving wheat. Where had she gone? He couldn't go after her if he didn't know which direction she'd taken.

Eventually he gave up and went inside to phone the commune.

Grace answered. She gave him a hard time because he hadn't called in months. "Don't tell me it's Brian, our friendly neighbour."

"Cut it out, Grace. I'm ringing about Agnes."

"What?"

"Agnes. She was here about half an hour ago. She looked sick."

"We don't have a goat called Agnes."

"Not a goat. A girl. Black hair. Light brown dress. She came across the river."

"Not from here, she didn't," said Grace.

"Maybe I got the name wrong. She had an accent. Scottish or Irish. I'm not sure."

"There's no one like that staying here."

"She's young. She looked pretty spaced out to me. You know — stoned."

"Brian, there are only the five of us. No visitors." Grace's voice had an edge to it. "Are you playing some kind of game?"

"No! Grace, I'm not trying to be nosy. I just want to make sure she gets back all right. I'm worried."

"Did she tell you she came from our community?"

"She didn't, but she walked from that direction. She was shivering and she kept calling me Freddy."

"Freddy?" Grace began to laugh. "You sure it's not you who's stoned?"

"There's nowhere else she could have come from," he insisted.

"Try your imagination," said Grace and she put down the phone.

He didn't know what to do. He sat on the back porch and picked up the shawl which was now almost dry. It was a grey triangle, knitted plain, with fringes on two sides. He put it to his face. It smelled of seaweed. He scratched his head and felt helpless. Whatever the cause, the girl was sick, and if she tried to go back over the river, she could slip again and . . . Maybe he should go and have a look.

With the sun and wind high, and dust blowing in his face, he took a long walk along the riverbank, poking in the weeds at the edge. He was thankful that he found nothing but a couple of beer cans and some plastic bags. Well, that was it then. He'd done all he could short of phoning the police. What was there to say to the cops? That a young junkie was wandering round the countryside? And he certainly wasn't going to tell his parents. He'd go back, have some lunch and forget about her.

But there was no forgetting. In fact, there was no space to think of anything else. He took the shawl to his room and hung it over a chair, and he heard her voice in his head, "Freddy Dysart! It's me, your Agnes."

He was glad when his parents came home. They arrived soon after five, hot in their town clothes and anxious to get changed.

"Shall I help unpack the car?" he said, forgetting.

His father spread his arms to bar the way. "You can help by going to your room, young fellow-me-lad," he said in a hearty voice.

"What? Oh. Sure."

"We won't be long, dear," said his mother. "We'll call when it's time to come out."

He had already seen the cardboard cartons filling the back seat. So they'd bought him a stereo system — huge speakers to anchor him home. It sure would be difficult to hitchhike into Christchurch with that lot.

He lay on his bed, the shawl spread across his chest. The wool was dry now but stiff and salty and feeling of her in a way he couldn't describe. It was as though he were holding her against him, so close that her eyes were laughing inside him, and his name really was Freddy.

When his mother knocked, he pushed the shawl under his pillow and sat up. "Come in."

She put her head round the door. "It's all right, now, Brian. Dad just wanted to get your present away."

He said, "Mum, wasn't your grandfather's name Dysart?"

"Yes. Arthur Dysart. Why?"

"Not Freddy Dysart?"

"No. Arthur Wallis Dysart and his wife's name was Margaret."

"Did he have a brother?"

"Grandpa? Goodness no! He was surrounded by women — two sisters, three daughters and five granddaughters."

"Do we have any Dysart cousins I don't know about? Any called Freddy?"

"No, but if you're interested I'll get the old photos out. It's funny. I was just thinking of them this afternoon. I was feeding a parking meter and suddenly they popped into my mind; Grandpa, Grandma, the farm, how I used to come here when I was little — "

He asked, "When did your grandfather buy the farm?"

"They moved here in the 1920's, just before the Depression. But he didn't buy it. He inherited it from his uncle. Oh, yes! That uncle's name was Frederick."

"Freddy?"

"I never heard anyone talk about him as Freddy. Frederick Dysart. He did very well for himself in the goldfields and bought this land when it was still standing bush, Grandpa said."

"Why didn't the land go to Frederick Dysart's children?"

"He was a bachelor. Never married. That's why Grandpa got it."

"Do you have any photos of him?"

"Grandpa?"

"No. Frederick."

"Oh, I wouldn't think so. Not that far back. I never heard much about him except for the story about why he never married. They say he was engaged to a girl in England. She was coming out to marry him but she got some illness and died on the boat. They buried her at sea."

Brian was still. It occurred to him that he should have felt surprise, but he didn't. It was as though someone was unwrapping a truth inside him which he had always known. He said to his mother, "Was her name Agnes?"

"Agnes? What makes you ask?"

"Was it?"

"I wouldn't have a clue what her name was. I didn't know you were all that interested in family history."

"I wondered if I looked like him — like Frederick."

"For heaven's sake, he died twenty years before I was born. But I suppose it's possible. You could be a throwback. You're a Dysart, not a McPhee, that's for sure." She stopped. "Who told you their names were Agnes and Freddy?"

He slid his hand under the pillow to touch the shawl. "I don't know, Mum, I think it was something I dreamed."

She frowned for a moment, then smiled. "Your father's made a pot of tea," she said.

That night, Brian was far from sleep. He stood in front of the mirror trying to find something about his face that was unfamiliar, something changed. He said, "Brian? Freddy?" trying the names as he would try on shirts to see if they fitted. They both did. He was Brian. He was Freddy. He didn't understand. But it was the name Agnes which evoked the deepest response. When he said it, his chest filled up with a pain that overflowed into his arms and his breathing hurt. And yet the pain was also pleasure. He looked at himself in the mirror and dared to think, I'm in love. No sooner had he admitted it than another thought rushed in unbidden. Love beyond the grave. He reflected on that without flinching. He thought he now knew who his visitor was. But who was he? Brian here and now? Or Freddy beyond the grave?

Whatever, the vision of the girl was with him to stay and her name settled like a full stop against the unfinished sentence of his life.

He tried to think of the problems which had possessed him, the failed exams, the job applications which were never answered, but each time the girl came between him and his disappointments, so they receded into the distance.

He lay on the bed with his face against her shawl, and at some time in the early hours of the morning, he heard her voice outside his window.

"Freddy Dysart? Be you awake in there?"

He was out of bed in an instant, running to the window and flinging it open.

She was standing in the moonlight in her wet dress, her face turned up to him, her arms raised. The smell of the sea filled the room.

"Agnes!"

"Freddy! Oh, dearest Freddy!" She laughed and clasped her hands together like a child. "Take me home!"

He leaned out of the window towards her. She was standing at the edge of the rose garden like some pale, moonwashed flower. Beyond her, the wheatfields shone clear to the horizon and on them, not far from the house fence, sat a tall ship with furled sails. He could see every detail of the deck and rigging.

"I'm coming!" he called to her and he drew back from the window.

Her smile went. "No, Freddy! Don't leave me!"

"I'm not! I'm going to the door. Be there in a minute."

Her cry went up like the wail of a seabird but he left the window and ran round his chair to the bedroom door. Before he got there, a strong gust slammed the window shut and howled across the chimney. He glanced at the window but kept going, down the darkened hall, out through the kitchen and round the outside of the house to his room.

She was not there.

The garden was buffeted by wind and the roses swayed, scraping branches. Out on the sea of rippling wheat, the ship was moving. The wind had filled its sails, which were as white as the moon itself, and it was gliding towards the horizon.

"Agnes!" He ran round the house, calling

her name. The light went on in his parents' room.

"Agnes! Agnes!"

There was nothing to hear except his father's voice somewhere behind him, and nothing to see but an ocean of wheat blowing in the wind.

Cottage by the Sea

Andrea decided that if parents could be rated on a scale of one to ten, these two would get a nine; one mark deducted for their habit of viewing everything through their occupations. Still, she thought, with one of them a mental health nurse and the other a schoolteacher, what could anyone expect?

They were both very interested in the dream that she had been having, off and on, for nearly a year. Whenever she sat down to breakfast, one of them, usually Dad, started conversation with, "Did you visit the cottage again last night?" If she had, they would pounce on the details as though this were the latest cryptic crossword.

"Certain dream symbols are common to all people," said Dad.

Andrea reached for the muesli. "What's a symbol?"

"Something that stands for something else," said Mum.

Dad was about to pour coffee on his toast. He looked just in time and transferred the coffee pot to his cup. "A house, for example, usually represents yourself or your body. The kind of house is very important. It says a lot about self-image."

Andrea shrugged. "This house is little and about a hundred years old. I'm tall and thirteen."

"An only child can be older than her years," said Dad. "She's heir to generations of family tradition and responsibility."

"I don't know about that," said Andrea, "I just keep thinking I know this house for real. I reckon I visited it when I was too young to remember."

"Are there trees round it?" Dad asked.

"No, it's too sandy. Right on the beach. There's a wooden fence that's just been put up. It isn't painted."

"Need for privacy," Dad said.

"The walls are white weatherboard and there's a red iron roof with a TV aerial.

Once I saw a seagull sitting on the aerial and choking down a whole fish."

Mum said, "As far as I know, it isn't part of your early childhood experience. What do you say, Paul?"

"Everything's a part of early experience," he said, waving his coffee cup. "It depends on what images we use to interpret that experience."

"Maybe it goes back further," said Andrea. "It could just be that I lived in this cottage in a past life and now I'm remembering it in my sleep."

"A TV aerial from a past life?" Mum asked.

"Trees in a dream," said Dad, "usually indicate relationships. Friends and family."

"I said no trees."

"None?"

"Just a little garden with lavender and geranium bushes."

Dad smiled and leaned back in his chair. "Well, that's nice."

"I wouldn't mind a cottage by the sea," Mum said, packing up the exam papers. "It sure would beat camping."

"The sea represents our deepest energies," said Dad. "It's our primeval fluid."

Andrea pushed her plate away. "Oh, come off it, Dad. I didn't make up this house. It's a dream but it's real. Like a memory. The only things that change in it are the people. I used to see an old couple. Then it was a family of young kids. Now the house is empty."

"It'll be interesting to see if you still dream about it when you're on holiday," Mum said. "A break from routine can mean a change in sleep and dream patterns. It's a pleasant dream, isn't it?"

"Oh yes. I love going there."

"If I were you I wouldn't worry about it," Dad said, patting her hand.

"I don't worry about it. It's you two who think —"

"Yoiks!" said Mum, looking at her watch. "As from five minutes ago, I'm not here. Where's my bag? End of term is hell. I'll be glad when we can pitch tent in the middle of nowhere — and that's my dream."

Andrea watched her parents being swept into the whirlpool of a working morning, racing around, looking for papers, socks, lists, car keys. She realized that they were trying to fit her experience into their lives and they would probably never realize what it meant to her. She wondered if she should stop talking about her visits to the cottage by the sea.

The dream persisted over the holidays, in spite of her mother's suggestion that it might disappear. There was nothing during the week of Christmas, but on New Year's Day when they were camping on the shores of Lake Taupo, it came again.

It was a hot afternoon and Andrea had sprawled out in the tent on top of her sleeping bag to read a book. The print blurred, her head drooped, and then, with a quick feeling of pleasure, she was on the yellow sand beach walking towards the cottage which was set on the other side of a couple of low sandhills spiked with flowering lupin and marram grass. She went through the paling gate which was exactly opposite the back door and separated from it by a path of crushed shells. On either side were borders of lavender, and geraniums as bright as fire engines.

As she entered the back porch, something remote in her was saying, "Mum and Dad don't believe this is real. I have to prove it to them," and it became important to her that everything she saw be catalogued. She was in the lean-to at the back of the house, the space shared by the kitchen, bathroom and laundry. Above the kitchen bench there was a row of tiles, white with green lilies on them. Two of the tiles were cracked. The electric stove was old but above it, on a metal shelf, was a fairly new microwave oven that looked out of place. There was a kitchen dresser against the opposite wall, a cracked table with turned legs and four wooden chairs painted pink. The rug near the table was made of strips of cloth plaited and stitched into a flat spiral. Apart from that and the hall runner, the floor was bare. Once the boards had been varnished but they were now worn to patches of grey wood.

She entered the back bedroom, knowing she would find two small beds, a painted chest of drawers and a wardrobe with a curtain over it. But there was something new in the room, a small boy lying on one of the beds, his thumb in his mouth. He stared at her. She backed away.

For such a small cottage, the hall was wide, like the aisle of a church. There was a patterned strip of red and green carpet down the middle, with chairs and a coat rack at the side. The front door was of heavy, dark varnished panels with a brass lock and long, narrow panes of rippled glass. To the right of the door was another bedroom. It had a black iron bed with a green satin eiderdown and on the wall was an old Victorian picture of two children playing with a little dog in a doll's pram.

Opposite the bedroom was the living room, which had a collection of shells lined up on the window ledge. There was a television set in the room, a couch and several chairs. As Andrea stood there, a woman suddenly rose from one of the chairs. She was young, with long hair and bare feet and she was holding a magazine. She stared at Andrea and said, "Who are you?"

Andrea woke up.

The sun was shining against the wall of the tent and she felt hot and irritable. It was the first time that anyone had spoken to her in her dream. She was sure that if she had stayed asleep, she and the woman could have had a conversation and she might have found out something about the cottage. She closed her eyes but could not return.

During the next week, as they travelled south, she dreamed of the cottage again but this time there was no one in it.

They were at the Waikanae camping ground for her mother's birthday on the ninth of January. She and Dad planned the evening meal together and early in the day went to the township to shop. The back seat of the car was soon filled with plastic bags: fresh strawberries, three massive steaks, a bottle of wine, a straw hat decorated with dried flowers, a beach towel, a birthday card.

On the way back to the camping ground, Dad took a wrong turning and they ended up near the beach. As he was cruising along, his head out the window looking for signposts, they passed the cottage.

Andrea knew it instantly, even though she was now seeing it from the road. Recognition sounded like a bell inside her.

There were the white weatherboards, the red iron roof with the aerial, the fence, the front door with its panes of rippled glass.

"Dad, that's it! That's the cottage I dream about!"

He stopped and put the car in reverse. The paling fence loomed large beside her window and she saw a red and white land agent's sign on it.

"The one for sale?"

"Yes. It's the same place! Come and look!"

She took him by the hand, in such a hurry that she almost dragged him through the gate. Round the side of the house they went and out to the back, which faced the sandhills and the beach. She showed him the shell path, the beds of geranium and lavender.

"I told you I didn't make it up. Now do you believe me?"

"Are you sure it's the same place?"

"Yes. Yes, yes, yes!"

For once he had no answer. He stood on the path, scratching his head while she tried the back door. It was locked. So was the front.

"I want you to see inside," she said. "You'll find everything's exactly the way I described it."

He started walking up the side of the house, stopping to peer in at the kitchen window which was blanketed with a heavy lace curtain. "I wonder if the land agent is home?" he said.

Not only was the land agent home, he was willing to come round immediately. As he fitted a key into the front door, Andrea whispered to her father, "Brass lock. The door's varnished inside."

She felt that she should have led the way but it was the land agent who went first, describing the cottage in a magnified voice.

"You are not going to believe the price!"

"The whole thing is unbelievable," Dad murmured.

"Wait for it!" cried the man. "Only half of the government valuation. An incredible, tiny twenty-seven thousand dollars!"

"What did you say?" Dad asked.

"Two, seven, oh, oh, oh. Twenty-seven thousand, which wouldn't even buy the land in a place like this."

"What's wrong with it?"

"Nothing. Not a single thing. Part of an estate, you see. Family have had tenants in but now they want it sold. Urgent sale, insane price. Someone's going to get the bargain of a lifetime."

"At that price there has to be something wrong with it."

"Wrong, sir? It's faultless. Stand any inspection. If it were mine I'd replace the stove but that's nothing. Come and look at the kitchen."

Andrea whispered, "There are white tiles with green lilies on them."

Dad looked at every part of the house and garden, then said to Andrea, "I think your mother should see this."

She grabbed his arm. "Are you going to buy it?"

He hushed her and glanced at the land agent. "All I'm saying is your mother should look at it."

"Don't leave it too late to make a decision," said the man. "It's only just on the market. My bet is it won't last two days."

As he drove away, a woman who was

weeding a garden on the other side of the road, called out, "Have you been looking at the cottage?"

"Yes," said Dad.

"Did he tell you it's just gone on the market? Thought so. That notice has been up for nearly a year. No one will buy it."

Dad sighed. "I thought there had to be a catch."

The woman laughed and forked the sand round some daisies. "They can't give it away. They've had a succession of tenants in the meantime, but even those don't stay. One week. Two weeks — "

"What's wrong with it? Plumbing?"

"No," said the woman. "The house is haunted, that's what. There's this ghost — a young girl who walks through the place as though she owns it. Disappears into thin air. You wouldn't catch me living in that place, I can tell you!"

The Tale of Tarama

When the old chieftain died, two warriors in the village sought to take his place. Their names were Vaisi and Tarama, and they had competed with each other since childhood.

Some of the people preferred Vaisi. They said, "Vaisi must be our next chief. He will rule with his head and show great cunning."

"No," said the others. "Tarama is the only true leader. He will rule with his heart and be most wise."

Since there could be no agreement amongst the people, it was decided that Vaisi and Tarama would have a wrestling match. The winner would become the new chieftain of the tribe.

"That suits me," said Tarama, who was the stronger.

"I will wrestle," said Vaisi, "but not here. We'll go, just the two of us, to the forest of Rashiki-vo. We will fight by the river of brown stones."

"As you wish," said Tarama, and the two young men went into the dark forest.

At the edge of the river, Tarama unfastened his cloak of parrot feathers. As he stooped to lay it on the stones, Vaisi sprang at him and struck him a great blow on the head with a club. Tarama fell down dead.

"A leader should know how to look after his own interests," laughed Vaisi, as he rolled Tarama's body into the river. "Good-bye forever, Tarama."

A giant eel saw Tarama's body and ate it. The spirit of Tarama went into the eel and Tarama became the eel.

Tarama was pleased with his new body, which was fast and powerful. He soon learned the ways of the river, knew all the boulders and sunken branches, the muddy holes under the banks. He could slide over stones like a shadow. He could catch small trout in the floating weeds. On dark, wet nights he came out of the water and slithered through the forest to eat frogs and the eggs of woodhens.

Sometimes Rashiki-vo, the god of the forest, came to the river to talk with Tarama. "Are you happy in my forest, Tarama?" he'd ask.

"Four parts happy," Tarama would reply.

"That is good," Rashiki-vo would say.

One afternoon, Rashiki-vo said, "Are you happy, Tarama?" and the eel replied in a distant voice. "Three parts happy and one part sad."

"Why is that?" said Rashiki-vo.

"I have unfinished business to attend to," sighed Tarama. "Back in my village." And Tarama told Rashiki-vo about Vaisi.

"Revenge is not a good thing," said Rashiki-vo. "It hurts both giver and receiver. Forget about Vaisi and the wrong he has done you."

But Tarama could not forget. The need for revenge possessed him and, finally, Rashiki-vo told him to go to his village and settle the matter.

"I will help you all I can," Rashiki-vo said. "But remember that you go with my warning."

The next morning, Rashiki-vo sent a fantail to flutter over the river above Tarama's lair. The eel leaped from the water and grabbed the small bird by the tail.

"Let me go! Let me go!" squeaked the fantail.

"On one condition," said Tarama. "You will fly to the village and tell everyone there is a giant eel in the river."

"But people will catch you!" said the fantail.

"Do as I say," ordered Tarama, "or I will pull you under the water and you will drown."

"I will do it," cried the fantail and it flew away to the village.

Before the day had ended, a fisherman came to the river with a spear and a net.

Tarama rose to the surface. "Catch me! Catch me!" he sang.

When the fisherman saw the size of the eel, he shook with fear and greed.

"Catch me! Catch me!" Tarama sang again, and he leaped towards the fisherman's spear.

The fisherman could not believe his luck, but he was still afraid of this creature. It didn't squirm and writhe on the bank but lay quietly in the reeds, looking up at him and singing in a faint voice, "Take me to the wife of Vaisi, your chief."

Disappointed, but not daring to do otherwise, the fisherman hoisted the eel over his shoulder, took it to the village and presented it to Vaisi's wife.

"What a great eel!" she cried. "Put it down beside the fire."

As soon as the fisherman put down the eel it cried, "Cook me! Cook me!"

So Vaisi's wife placed it on the red hot coals and cooked it.

"Eat me! Eat me!" Tarama sang.

"I should keep you for my husband's supper," said the woman.

But Tarama kept singing, "Eat me! Eat me!" so Vaisi's wife ate the eel. At once the spirit of Tarama went into the child she was carrying and Tarama became her unborn baby.

Some months later there was a big celebration in the village for the chief's wife who had given birth to a fine son. What a proud man was Vaisi. He couldn't bear to let the baby out of his sight. As the child grew, Vaisi took him everywhere, lavishing gifts and attentions on him. He never grew tired of boasting about him.

"See how fast and strong he is," he'd say. "He runs like a wild young thing of the forest, and swims as though he were born in the river."

Years went by. The boy grew to be a man and was his father's constant companion. Since Vaisi was becoming feeble with age, it was agreed in the village that his son should be the next chieftain.

One day, the young man was in the forest, hunting wild pig for his father. He heard a voice calling, "Tarama! Tarama!" a name that he had almost forgotten. He turned and recognised Rashiki-vo.

"You have been too long away from the river," said Rashiki-vo. "It is time to return. Have you finished what you wanted to do?"

Tarama shook his head.

"I will give you one more day," said Rashiki-vo.

Tarama spent the rest of his time with Vaisi, who recognised sadness in the young man. "My son, your heart carries more weight than it can bear. What is wrong?"

Tarama sat down beside Vaisi and struggled for an answer.

"Are you worried about being the new chief?"

48

Tarama said, "How did you become chief, Father?"

"I was chosen by the people as you have been," said Vaisi.

Tarama said, "I heard there was some kind of contest."

Vaisi shook his head. "You heard in error, my son. It is true we were going to have a wrestling match but the other man was a coward. He refused to fight. He ran away into the forest and no one ever saw him again."

"That is not how I remember it," said Tarama, and he told Vaisi the story of his lives.

At first Vaisi would not believe it. But when his son described every detail of the killing by the river, he knew that the tale could not be made up. He moaned and covered his head and lay on the ground, crying, "Oh, what have I done to you? What have I done? Kill me now, my son!"

Tarama lifted Vaisi and held him. "No, Father. It is true that I did plan to kill you. You taught me how to hate and I was full of bitterness. But now, Father, you've taught me how to love. I cannot kill you. Neither can I stay here. Rashiki-vo was right. Revenge is not a good thing."

"You are not going away!" cried Vaisi.

Tarama nodded. "I have no choice."

"No!" Vaisi clutched at him. "You are all I have! Do not leave me!"

Tarama put his hands on the old man's shoulders and gently touched his forehead with his own. "Goodbye, Vaisi. Remember that I go one part happy and three parts sad."

"My life is finished if you leave me!" Vaisi shouted.

But Tarama had already turned away. He ran, heavy of heart, to the forest of Rashiki-vo and the river of brown stones where a giant eel waited for him.

The Well

When the ambulance brought Grandpa home, Mum said, "He's back with his family but he's still sick. So no shouting, okay? No running like mad things down the hall."

Tara said, "When's he going to get better?"

"I don't know," said Mum.

Henry, who had been listening to adult talk, said, "Grandpa's going to die."

Mum didn't say anything but Aunty Kath crouched down and put her hands on the children and said, "Yes, he wants to die in his own home."

The next morning, after the doctor had been, they were allowed to go in and see Grandpa briefly. They didn't like being in the room, which was dark and smelling of bad breath, and they didn't know what to say to him. The man in the bed didn't look like Grandpa. He was boney and yellow and when he talked he coughed. The only thing about him that was still strong was his gaze. He turned his eyes on them, huffed and crackled, and said, "How are my ratbags?"

More relatives came that afternoon and the house was too full for Henry and Tara, who played outside. Even their back-yard spaces were taken up by uncles who cooked pots of mussels on a fire near the clothesline and drank homebrew while they talked about their work. The only place left was the orchard, which was normally forbidden because of the old well, but no one was minding too much about things like that. For a while, Tara and Henry stayed at the safe end of the orchard. They played in the plum trees, throwing green plums at the cat and tying a rope to a low branch for a swing. But the well was always there at the edge of their sight and, eventually, having explored everything else, they found themselves looking at the old wooden well-cover weighted down with bricks.

Henry said, "I've never seen down there in my whole life."

"Me neither," replied Tara. "Grandpa said he'd wallop us."

Henry looked at her. She looked back but they didn't put the thought into words.

"Do you think there are ghosts in here?" said Henry as he began moving bricks.

"Nah!"

"Might be a wishing well," he said.

The wooden cover was heavier than it looked. It had to be pulled backwards, so there was no danger of them falling in, and it kept getting stuck, but then it suddenly came away and they sat down hard on the bricks they'd put behind them. Tara was the first to look down the well. "Told you there weren't any ghosts," she said.

There wasn't much else, either. As a well, it was a bit of a disappointment. Tara had thought that wells should be round but this was square with boards lining the sides. The boards were black with damp and had white fungus growing in the cracks. It went a long way down but didn't have much water in it. When they dropped in a brick it splashed, then settled with its top above the surface.

"Doesn't look like a wishing well, either," said Henry.

Tara lay on the ground with her face down the well. "I wish for Grandpa not to die," she said. But nothing happened. There wasn't even an echo.

Henry had some green plums in his pocket. They watched those splash and bob. Then they heard Aunty Kath and Uncle Peter calling them. They jumped back and ran to the other side of the orchard, wriggled through the fence, raced up the side path and pretended they had been playing near the vegetable garden. Uncle Peter looked at them with eyes like Grandpa's. "You two keep out of trouble," he said.

Nearly all the aunts and uncles were sitting in Grandpa's room, with only Aunty Kath and Uncle Peter in the kitchen getting the dinner. Tara heard Aunty Kath on the phone telling someone her father was in a coma.

Later, when Tara and Henry were sitting under the table with the cat, she asked, "What's a coma?"

Henry said, "It's one of those curvy things. You know — you put it in a sentence when you want to have a breath."

Tara put her face against the cat. "I think it means dying."

Henry sat up straight, taking a quick breath. "The well! We left the cover off!"

"No one can get drowned," Tara said.

"Yeah, but if they see it they'll know it was us. We'll be in a heap of trouble. Come on. We'd better go out and put it back."

"It's heavy!" moaned Tara.

"Quick! Before it gets dark!" insisted Henry.

The orchard was full of long shadows and the grass was already wet with dew. As they drew near the well, they heard a woman's voice. "Is there anyone there?"

Tara jumped. Henry immediately dropped down on his hands and knees in the long grass, and looked towards the house.

"Are you there?" the voice said again. It was coming from the well.

Tara said, "Someone's fallen in!"

The woman in the well was no one they knew. She was sort of fat, with fair hair and freckles on her face and a white apron over a red cardigan. On the bib of her apron was a nurse's badge. The rest of her they couldn't see, for it was stuck at the bottom of the well.

"Did you fall in?" Henry asked.

"I rather think I was wished in," the woman said. "Get me a rope, will you?"

"There's one on the swing," said Henry. "Wait here!"

"I'm not going anywhere," the woman laughed.

Henry ran off to the plum tree and Tara lay on her stomach to talk to the woman. "Were you coming to see our Grandpa?"

"I was."

"I could tell," said Tara. "I saw your nurse's badge."

"A midwife, in fact," said the woman. "How far away is that rope?"

"Not far. My brother's getting it now. His name's Henry and I'm Tara."

The woman smiled again. "Pleased to meet you, Tara. I'm Death. Be a sweetie and tell him to hurry."

"He's coming. He's hurrying. What's a midwife-in-fact?"

"Oh. Midwife? That's someone who helps with a birth."

"But you said you came to see Grandpa."

"I did. He's in labour. He needs me urgently."

"But our Grandpa is dying."

"Same thing. Oh good!" The woman was looking at Henry who had appeared beside Tara with the rope. "Tie one end to a strong tree and throw the other to me."

Henry did that. One end of the rope went round a quince tree, the other end was lowered down the well. It should have reached the woman but it didn't fall straight. It looped and curled across the well so that it stayed out of her reach. Henry pulled it up and tried again. The same thing happened.

"Just what I thought!" said the woman, looking annoyed. "I got wished in here. Have you two been wishing?"

"We thought it was a wishing well," said Tara.

"All wells are wishing wells," sighed the woman. "I suppose you wished your grandfather wouldn't die."

"Yes," said Tara.

"Well, that leaves him and me in a right old pickle. You can throw that rope all you like but it won't reach me."

"We'll get our uncles," said Henry.

"No good either," said the woman. "People like that can't see me. They'll look in here, see an empty well and punish you for telling lies."

"But we see you," said Tara.

"You're children. You haven't decided yet what you want to see and don't want to see. Most adults refuse to see Death."

"What about Grandpa?" Tara asked.

"Oh, he'll see me all right. He asked me to come."

Henry, who had come late to the conversation, was looking bewildered.

Tara said, "This lady is Death. She's come to take Grandpa away."

"Huh?" Then Henry laughed. "You're kidding."

"That's an unusual word for it," said the woman.

"I saw a picture of Death on a horse," said Henry. "Death is a skeleton with a scythe in its hands."

The woman sighed. "You are not describing Death, but people's fears. Tell me, do I look like a skeleton?"

"She's a midwife-in-fact," said Tara.

The woman looked from one to the other. "Do you know where babies come from?"

"Sure," said Henry. "A baby grows in its mother's womb."

"Then it gets born," said Tara.

Death said, "I'll tell you a little story to help you understand. This earth is your mother and your body is her womb."

"My body?" said Tara.

"That's silly," Henry said.

Death shook her head. "You live in your body but you don't own it. It belongs to earth. You grow in it for as long as you need it. When you're born, you leave it behind like a chicken leaving its egg. But there is one problem. People can't leave their bodies without me to help them. Which is why I must get out of this well at once."

"You can't take our Grandpa," said Henry.

"He's tired of waiting. He's saying to himself, 'Where is that confounded woman?' Actually, he used a stronger word than that but you don't need to know what it is."

Henry stepped back from the well. "I don't believe this stuff."

"That doesn't change anything," said Death. "I have to get out of here and only a wish will do that. You can't have more than one wish. If you two wished me in here, I'll need another child to wish me out. Do you have any brothers or sisters?"

"No," said Henry.

"Henry can do it!" said Tara. "He didn't wish for Grandpa not to die. I did that on my own!"

"Good grief!" said the woman. "Why didn't you tell me that before? Henry, all you have to do is reverse Tara's wish and I'll be out of here in two ticks."

Henry was silent.

"Henry?"

"I don't want Grandpa to die," he said.

"Your grandfather wants it. He's getting very impatient and so am I. How would you like to be down here with your feet in cold water?"

"Tara? Henry?" Uncle Peter and Uncle Barry were coming across the orchard.

"Are you kids playing by that old well?"

There was no time to say anything else to Death. They stepped backwards away from the well as their uncles came through the long grass, shouting at them.

"The cover's off!" cried Uncle Peter.

Uncle Barry was looking down the well. "Plums!" he said. "And what were you doing with that rope?"

Henry said, "You can't see plums! She's in — !"

"Green plums!" yelled Uncle Barry, throwing the rope aside. "You've thrown a brick down there, too."

Tara and Henry looked at each other.

Uncle Peter had the well cover and was putting it over the hole. "Damned kids," he was muttering. "Turn your back for a minute — "

"Get back to the house!" Uncle Barry said to them. "If I catch either of you in this orchard again, you're going to be really sorry for yourself. Go on, what are you standing there for?"

There was nothing they could do except go back to the kitchen where some of the adults were sitting and talking.

Mum looked at them. "You kids still up? Wash your feet. Do your teeth. Go to bed."

"Can we go outside again?"

"No! Bed!"

Aunty Kath came in from the front room and said, "He's still the same."

"Tough old rooster," someone said. "Never did give in easy."

Mum got mad with Tara and Henry. "What are you two big ears standing there for? Didn't you hear me?"

They still hung about the table, picking up bits of cake, but when Uncle Peter and Uncle Barry came in, they went quickly to the bathroom.

Uncle Barry's voice was loud. "Little beggars took advantage. Even had a rope over the side."

In bed, Tara said, "Why didn't you wish?"

"I didn't want to," said Henry.

"She'll be cold," said Tara. Then after a while she asked, "Can people sleep standing up?"

Henry said, "We'll wait until everyone's in bed."

"You're going to wish?"

"No. We'll just take the top off and she can get herself out."

They tried to stay awake but couldn't. When Tara next opened her eyes, birds were chirping and the window was grey with light. She shook Henry. "The well! The well!"

They went out in their pyjamas, got halfway across the orchard and stopped. On top of the well cover was a large block of old concrete, so heavy that even when they pushed together, they couldn't move it. They went back to the house.

Throughout the day, people came and went from Grandpa's room and spoke in whispers to each other, saying things like, "How can he go on like that?" or "I'd hoped to stay for the funeral but I've got to get back to work," or "At least he can't feel anything."

Henry and Tara thought about Grandpa, but even more, they thought of Death down the well.

"You should have wished," Tara said.

"There's no way of moving that concrete," said Henry.

"She hasn't got anything to eat down there."

"She can't die. She's Death. Stop worrying about her."

But for all his talk, Henry was as concerned as Tara. That afternoon one of the neighbours took them out to a farm where they rode horses and ate icecream but they were too preoccupied to enjoy it. Henry whispered, "It was you who put her there in the first place!"

Another night passed, and most of another day. Grandpa's breathing could be heard all over the house, a rough, bubbling sound that Aunty Kath said was more than she could take. She switched the television on. "I don't know why he's fighting it," she said to Uncle Peter.

Henry and Tara both saw the news that night. Aunty Kath called the others. "Guess what? There's been no recorded death in New Zealand or Australia these last two days. Information is coming in from other countries. They think it's something to do with solar flares."

"What nonsense!" snorted Uncle Barry and he turned off the television. They were all quiet for a moment and Grandpa's breathing came loud through the wall.

"It's just coincidence," Uncle Barry said.

An hour or so later, Henry and Tara sneaked into the orchard and crawled through the long grass to the well. Henry leaned over that part of the lid which wasn't covered by the concrete block. He said in a loud whisper, "Are you still there?"

"I am," said Death, her voice surprisingly loud.

"We can't move the cover. Our uncles put a big weight on it."

"You have to do something!" Death answered. "It's not just your grandfather. There are millions. They're all calling and I can't hear myself think. I've got a world crisis on my hands."

"Can I make a wish out here?" Henry asked.

"No. It's not a well out there. You have to be in the same position your sister was in when she made her wish."

"But we can't get the cover off!"

"Get your uncles to move it," Death said.

"They won't!" cried Henry.

"Find a way," said Death, "and find it fast."

Tara went to Uncle Barry. "You know when Henry and I were playing by the well — "

Uncle Barry glared at her.

"I dropped my bracelet down it."

"Tough," he said.

Tara said, "It was the gold one Grandpa gave me."

The uncles went into the orchard with a torch, a rope and an extension ladder. They pushed back the block of concrete and took off the lid. "Stand right back," they said to Tara and Henry.

Tara had already seen the woman down there. She looked a bit angry but was otherwise all right. She stood there with her arms folded and her mouth thin. "About time!" she said. Then she nodded towards the uncles. "It's all right. They can't see or hear me."

"I'm sorry," Tara said.

Uncle Barry waved his torch at her. "I should jolly well think so. Stand further back."

Henry called down to Death. "I'm going to wish now. Is here all right?"

Uncle Barry said, "No! I told you to stay well back!" and at the same time Death said, "No! Closer! You must wish right into the well."

Henry looked at his uncles who were shining their torches over Death's face. "Can't see anything down there but plums," said Uncle Barry.

Henry said quickly, "I think I can see it!" He dropped down on his stomach at the edge of the well and before they could blast him he pointed at Death.

"Where? Where?" said Uncle Peter, focussing the torch on Death's nose.

"Do it!" Death shouted at Henry.

And Henry said down the well, "I wish for Grandpa to die."

As the last word came out, Death vanished and Henry found himself staring down at some wrinkled green plums which floated near an almost submerged brick.

"What'd you say?" asked Uncle Peter.

"Nothing," said Henry, crawling backwards on his elbows.

"I just remembered," said Tara with a nervous laugh. "I left my bracelet in my room."

When they got back into the house, they found everyone crying and hugging each other and Aunty Kath said to Uncle Peter, "Your father's gone."

Uncle Peter put his arms around her. "That's a blessed relief," he said.

Aunty Kath was talking on the phone again. Right behind her, standing by the fireplace with her arm on the mantelpiece, was Death. She was smiling at Henry and Tara and now they could see all of her. Her shoes were wet and stained with mud and her hair was messed up as though she'd just got out of bed, but she didn't look bad considering she'd just spent two days in a well. She said, "I popped back to let you know how it went. He had a long hard labour but it was a quick and easy birth. He's thrilled to bits about it." She waved. "Have to go now. I'll see you again — but not for a long time."

Henry gave her a small wave. Tara said, "I'm really sorry about — you know — what you've had to put up with."

"Oh, that's all right," said Death and with another smile, she disappeared.

At the same time, everyone in the room stopped talking and looked at Tara and Aunty Kath said, "Why, bless the child! What an odd remark!"

Beyond the River

Soon after sunrise he unfastened the wet moorings and pushed the boat into the river.

The morning was fragile with frost and cold; the sun had lifted the mists from the water but was not warm enough to unwrap the whiteness that covered the scrub-rough banks. Ice crackled like cellophane under his boots.

First one leg, then the other. He moved slowly, for this morning he was feeling his age. His joints had been stiffened by seventy-six winters, his skin hardened by as many summers. Pressing his hands to his face, he breathed hard several times to loosen his fingers, then he took the oars from the bottom of the boat and fitted them — slowly, slowly — into the row-locks.

"Silly old fool," he said to the boat. "If you had any sense you'd still be in bed. Make do with spuds and bacon." He smiled and raised the oars.

The river was sluggish, the air still, and the first cut of the blades shattered both into bright splinters, but as the boat pulled upstream, the repetition grew monotonous, dip and drip and dip, till the sound became part of the silence and the river.

He knew this stretch of water so well it was no longer a friend but rather a part of his life which he accepted without gratitude, like breathing and sleeping. From it he took fish and firewood and occasional fowl, and in return he forgave it its many moods. Sometimes it brought, without warning, floods that smashed his boat and left a mess of debris in his one-roomed hut. Other times, in a teasing mood, it would tangle his carefully set eel lines into knots which defied his old fingers. But this morning the river was at its best; quiet, smooth as glass.

Round the first bend.

Although he'd turned the collar of his

tartan shirt up to his ears and pulled his knitted cap down to meet it, the cold still cut his face. It drew blood to his cheeks and puckered his eyes with water. On the bottom of the boat a thin film of ice had broken round the heels of his gumboots. By his right boot, lying on a bundle of sacks, was his rifle, a .22 five-shot repeater.

Past the second bend.

Here the river widened to a milky reflection of the sky. The trees and scrub along one bank fell into swamp where a stream spread itself under a mat of rushes and tussock grass to meet the main flow. Here the air moved with the sounds of wild things; the raupo rustled, bubbles burst and rippled, eels popped from hidden holes as the boat came near.

A duck broke cover and took off across the water, moving lazily. He watched until it was lost somewhere in the scrub, then he unbuttoned his shirt pocket and took out a slice of bread. He broke it and set it afloat on the river, then waited with the rifle across his knees as the bread drifted slowly down towards the rushes.

Movement. A splash of colour. Before he could raise his gun, the duck was gone, sinking half the bread in its wake. He waited. The raupo stirred and there it was again. No, a different bird. This time, a dun-coloured female. He bent forward along the barrel, elbow on knee. It swam warily against the reeds, brown against brown, head on one side, cautious.

He waited.

The duck grabbed a piece of bread and prepared for flight. Nothing happened. Further from the protection of the raupo it came, then hunger overcame suspicion.

He shot it.

Echoes. Echoes and cries and the beating wings of twenty, perhaps thirty birds. He didn't fire again. He put the rifle back in the boat and shaded his eyes, up one bank and down the other, looking and listening into the morning beyond the river. The quiet came back. There was no one. Nothing but a feeble movement in the rushes where the bird struggled, brown feathers and the water brown with blood. He paddled across, lifted it, dripping and quite dead, into the boat, and he grunted with satisfaction as his fingers spread under the breast feathers.

"She'll do." He threw the carcass down by his feet, wiped his hands and tucked them under his arms to ease the cold.

It was then that the other duck came back. He heard it before he saw it, a harsh cry and the sweep of wings, so sudden and so close that he put his arms over his head without thinking. Then, as he peered through his shirt sleeves, he saw the blue-green feathers, the outstretched neck and the wingtips only inches from his face.

"Clear off!" He waved his arms. "Go on, get out of it!"

The drake floated up high above his head, then turned and swooped low over the boat, up and over, each time calling to the heap of brown feathers. It showed no fear.

He tried to hit it with an oar, almost swamping the boat in the effort, and twice he grabbed at it as it settled in the water near him. There was always the rifle but he didn't want to shoot it. He killed only what he could eat.

"Get away, will you?"

It left the boat as soon as he started rowing. At the first bite of the oars it climbed up and away and followed in high, crying circles some distance behind him. Without breaking the rhythm of the stroke, he leaned forward, pulled the cap further over his ears and cursed the cold.

On and on, and still it followed. When he reached the last stretch and could see over his shoulder the smudge of smoke from his hut, he shipped oars and waited. Dart-shaped and dark against the pale frost sky it came, calling, calling, and down on the wind of its wings until it was swimming beside the boat.

He lifted the rifle and aimed.

How he missed at that range, he'd never know. The bird fell sideways and spun round in the water, trailing a wing. He fired again, this time through the neck.

Gradually the pattern of ripples flattened out round the small bundle of feathers. As the current moved the drake out midstream, he picked up the duck from the bottom of the boat and threw it after its mate.

Long after they had disappeared, he sat there. Now it was quiet again. No noise but the dripping of the oars and the slow, slow breathing of the river.

Moonwater and the Firestones

It had been said that when winter changed to summer, the warrior, Greysand, would go into battle and be killed. Greysand and his wife, Moonwater, lived with the prophecy through a long and cold winter, then, when the birds called for mates and the mountain rivers ran full, there was news of war.

Greysand received the order that he must fight. He and Moonwater told their families about the prophecy and then Greysand prepared not only for battle but also for his death. Both families went into mourning. The men cut themselves with shells and put thorns into their arms. The women covered their skin with ashes and refused to eat. The wailing in the village was like that of a colony of seabirds over a fishing ground.

Only Moonwater refused to accept Greysand's fate. She went to visit the Seer-of-all-things who lived by the river.

The old man knew at once why she had come. "Is it that time already?" he said.

"Wise One, is there any way I can save my husband?"

"There is," said the Seer-of-all-things. "If Greysand wears a necklace of firestones into battle, neither spear nor club can harm him."

"Firestones!" cried Moonwater.

"They are strong enough to turn aside the prophecy, even death."

"But, Wise One, it is impossible to get firestones. They are found only on top of the black glass mountain. People say that anyone who goes near the mountain is eaten by the monster, Grimako."

"I know of a way it can be done," said the Seer-of-all-things. "It is very dangerous and your chances of success are not good."

"What is it?" cried Moonwater.

"You will probably die," he warned.

"Without Greysand I am half dead anyway," she replied. "Tell me!"

The old man pointed. "In the middle of the river is an island and on it grows a giant flax bush. Cut the leaves and weave a basket and then travel quickly to the north. Go through the Forest of the Dead. Do not stop to look left or right but sing as you go."

"Sing?" said Moonwater. "What do I sing?"

"Whatever is in your heart. If that is good and true, the monster who guards the base of the mountain will sleep. You see, Grimako lacks knowledge of good, therefore all goodness is invisible to it. So sing your song of love and courage and hope and you will climb all the way to the top of the mountain without waking Grimako. You will find the firestones in a hollow where the mountain meets the sky. Fill your basket as fast as you can and return the way you came. You will be able to make the necklace before your husband goes to battle."

"I shall start at once."

"Be very careful when you make the basket," said the Seer-of-all-things. "Do not cut yourself. Grimako can smell a single drop of blood miles away. No amount of singing will protect you if the creature catches the scent of your blood."

Moonwater waded across the river to the island and cut the flax. She trimmed the leaves and softened them with a pipi shell and then plaited her basket. But in her haste, she got a small cut on her finger. She washed the cut in the river and tied a strip of flax round it so that Grimako would not smell the blood. With her basket over her arm, she set out on the long journey north to the Forest of the Dead.

She came to the edge of the forest late in the afternoon, but inside it was as dark as night. The trees grew tall, so thick at the tops that no sunlight ever touched the forest floor. The earth had the smell of decay and it sucked at her feet as though it were trying to hold her, while strands of lichen, hanging from the trees, touched her like wet hair as she passed.

Moonwater sang loudly of love and courage as soft, phosphorescent shapes swirled about her and then sped away through the trees. These were the spirits of the dead on their way north and they were everywhere. Although Moonwater did not look to left or right, she was aware that the spirits were close by on either side. Some went quietly, slipping through the branches like pale candle-flame. Others still carried the pain of their dying and howled and shrieked, their shapes writhing like twisted rope.

Moonwater's heart beat fast but she thought of Greysand and her song was strong. At least the spirits gave the forest a little light. Without them she would have stumbled over logs or fallen into deep pools. She was grateful and that, too, came into her song.

After a long time she came to a place where the ground was hard and smooth and she could hear a sound that was like a deep bass to her singing. She realised she was hearing the slow, snoring breath of Grimako, the monster that guarded the mountain. She didn't see Grimako but very soon there rose in front of her a slope of black grass, which rose stark out of the trees and which reflected the soft flickering shapes of the spirits. Moonwater's song was of love and strength as she approached the mountain. The noise of the sleeping monster was loud and the air round Moonwater was warmed by its foul breath, but still she couldn't see it.

She began to climb.

The black grass was slippery. Moonwater clung to it like a fly, seeking small cracks and bubbles which would give her a foothold. The basket was pushed high up on her arm and her song was strained with effort as she went up the slope one hand at a time. Past the trunks of tall trees, up through branches and leaves and, finally, she was above the forest. In front of her the mountain peak rose black and sharp against the night sky and she could see a faint white glow on the summit which showed her the location of the firestones.

Moonwater was so tired that her song had become more of a gasp. Her legs felt weak, her arms ached. The flax bandage round her finger caught on a glass ledge. She did not see the flax fall away. Nor did she notice that the cut on her finger had begun to bleed again.

She was almost at the peak when a great roar sounded throughout the forest. The mountain shook. Splinters of black glass came loose and fell down the slopes, shattering as they tumbled. Moonwater's song faltered, choked by fear. She held on for her life and saw that her finger was bare and bleeding. She knew that Grimako had woken with the smell of blood.

The creature roared again. Moonwater climbed as fast as she could, while all round her the mountain shivered and cracked. The glow of the firestones was very close now, and as she pulled herself over the rim of the crater she saw them — hundreds of white pebbles shining like stars in the nest of the mountain, each pebble a ball of pale fire.

Quickly, Moonwater filled her basket.

Far below her, the top of the forest rocked like a stormy sea and the huge, scaly head of Grimako cleared the trees. Moonwater glanced down. She saw yellow eyes, which brightened when they caught sight of her. She saw sharp teeth encircling a mouth bigger than a doorway, and a set of huge claws, which reached out and slashed at the glass surface. The monster was hauling itself up the mountain with great speed.

Clutching the glowing basket, Moonwater crossed the top of the mountain and prepared to descend the opposite slope. She stopped. There was no slope. The other side of the mountain was sheer cliff, straight down to the forest floor. So this was why the Seer-of-all-things had told her to return the way she'd come. It was the only way, and it was blocked by a monster that would devour her. Moonwater was trapped.

Grimako reached the top. Roaring, it stretched its neck towards her and opened its mouth. She felt the blast of its breath and saw the rows of teeth. With a scream, she jumped off the mountain.

Down the black wall of the cliff she fell, her arms wrapped about the basket. She most certainly would have been killed had not the spirits helped her. They rushed towards her like a strong wind and lifted her up. She was carried through the sky, whirling and twirling over the forest, the basket of firestones clutched tightly against her.

The voices of the spirits howled in her ears. One voice she recognized. It belonged to Greysand's grandmother, who had died many years before.

"I want my grandson," wailed the voice. "Give me the firestones!"

"No!" said Moonwater and at the same time she felt a tug at the basket.

"Give them! Give them!" Greysand's grandmother had the edge of the basket and was pulling it.

"No! No!" Moonwater shouted.

"You will not keep my grandson from me-ee-ee-ee!"

They had a tug-of-war above the tree tops. Neither would let go. It was difficult for Moonwater to keep her grip on the basket. She was turned this way and that in the rushing wind, for the grandmother's spirit was very strong.

"Give me those firestones!"

The basket came open. One last great tug, and it tipped sideways. The firestones spilled over the forest. Down they spun, as white and bright as falling stars, to be lost in the trees.

Satisfied, the spirit of Greysand's grandmother let go. The noise of the other spirits dropped to a whisper and the wind lessened. Moonwater drifted down from the sky with her empty basket and landed in her village where Greysand was about to leave for battle.

Sadly, Moonwater confessed her failure. "They're all gone," she said, holding up her basket.

"No. Not all gone," said Greysand, reaching inside. "Look, there is one stone left, caught in the weave." He took out the stone which shone in the palm of his hand. "I shall wear this stone to war and I shall pray that I might be as brave as my wife."

Greysand went into battle with the stone on a thong about his neck. He was not killed. He received severe wounds but recovered to live for many years.

No one today knows what happened to the stone he wore. But each springtime, the other firestones may be seen scattered over the forest. They have become flowers, which shine as bright as snowflakes against the dark green trees.

At the same time of the year, the flowers on the flax bush unfold from their buds, stained a dark red from the cut on Moonwater's finger.

Rangi Tamahehe

Oh, that big boss rooster, Rangi Tamahehe.
He was like a watch-dog for people coming
to the house, stamping his feet on the drive
and oo-oo-oohing with his feathers flared
out and his yellow eyes making fighting
talk. One look at that big bonfire of a bird
and the visitor would back off, leaving
Rangi Tamahehe to flap his wings and crow
like a boxer who'd just won the world
heavyweight title.

Yet when Nanny went out there calling,
believe it or not, that rooster would shrink
to half his size and walk sideways until he
was leaning against her leg. She would pick
him up, saying, "That's my boy. That's my
Rangi," and stroke his red and yellow
feathers.

And you know, he'd just sit there under

her arm as though he were sick or some-thing.

But the rooster didn't care for Nanny's sons, Larry and Erueti, and they liked him about the same amount. Each time they came from town, they made jokes about the chopping block just to get Nanny wild. "Hey, Mum, when are you going to get rid of that hoha rooster? He'll be tough. You won't know if you're eating boiled rooster or boiled saucepan."

Well, they were jokes, true enough, to begin with, but when the boys came back for Christmas they had several set tos with Rangi Tamahehe and it got to be a state of war.

One lunch time, fancying a cheese omelette, Larry went up to the chook house but there was no way he could get near the egg boxes. The rooster came up, beating the air like some fiery demon and Larry, taking one look at those spurs and beak, went off to make himself a cheese sandwich instead. He reckoned that every time he took a mouthful the rooster crowed at him.

"I'm going to get that bird," he said to

his brother. "I mean it. I'm going to knock his blimmin' head off."

"Out of order, boy," laughed Erueti. "How can you say things like that about the old lady's darling?"

But Erueti was laughing on the other side of his face when Rangi bailed him up in the washhouse. The rooster planted himself in the doorway and no amount of yelling could shift him. His feathers were all on end and there was an evil shine to his yellow eye as he stamped on the concrete ready to charge. His beak was open; he seemed to be crowing without making a sound.

Erueti remembered the stick his mother used for getting clothes out of the copper. He grabbed it, and at the same moment Rangi Tamahehe attacked. Nanny had to come to the rescue.

Larry said later, "You had your chance. Why didn't you knock the living daylights out of him?"

"It's all right to talk now," grumbled Erueti, "but when you've got this big tipua right in your face, all you can do is put your hands over your eyes."

"We have to get rid of him," Larry said. "He's dangerous. I mean, he's going to turn on her one day and we won't be round to help."

"We'll do it while she's out," agreed Erueti. "We'll just bury him up the back and she'll think he's wandered off and ended up as someone's Christmas dinner."

"The trouble is, catching him."

"It'll have to be night time when he's on the perch. Throw a sack over him and — bingo!"

Larry shrugged. "The only problem with that is the old lady never goes out at night."

But they had forgotten Christmas Eve and midnight mass. Their mother never missed going to church on Christmas Eve. That would be their chance. They'd be able to give old Rangi Tamahehe a right Merry Christmas, bury him and clean up before the mass was half over.

On the afternoon of the twenty-fourth the rest of the family came from down south and the house was full of talk and kids playing with the first of their presents. One of the uncles brought up a big ham. Nanny sent the boys to the garden for vegetables while she fried up the breads, and they all ate out on the back lawn with old Rangi locked in the chook house. That didn't stop him from crowing. He knew the place was being invaded and he was letting everyone know who was boss.

When it was time to go to church, Larry and Erueti said they'd stay home and clean up.

"You come," said Nanny. "I'll clean up when we get back."

"We're giving it a miss this year," Larry said.

"You can't! You always go with me!" she insisted.

"We might go to church tomorrow," said Erueti. "Go on, Mum, you'd better hurry. You won't get a seat if you're late."

She wasn't feeling good about it, but she left with the others and the boys started on the dishes. As soon as the last car drove off, they were out the door with a torch, a sack and the axe. Erueti stood out in the yard in a patch of light from the porch, and touched up the axe with an oilstone, singing to the tune of Jingle Bells, "Rooster's dead, rooster's dead, dead and gone away . . ."

They went up to the chook house.

It was dark in there and warm with the dusty smell of feathers. When they opened the door, some of the chooks shifted sideways on their perches but soon settled down again. Old Rangi Tamahehe was nearest the door, all fluffed up, his head drawn against his body in sleep. Larry threw the sack over him and by the time the rooster woke up, it was too late. Larry had hold of him by the legs and the sack was over his head and wings. Old Rangi screeched like a siren but he was helpless.

The noise brought all the hens off their perches, squawking and fluttering like crazy in the dark, feathers everywhere. Larry and Erueti backed out; Erueti shut the door. He took the axe and torch and guided the way back to the house and the woodheap at the end of the porch. He set up the torch so it shone down on the chopping block, an old macrocarpa log crisscrossed with axe marks. "You ready?" he said, shouldering the axe.

The rooster must have known his number was up because he suddenly went quiet and still, the way he did when Nanny picked him up. Holding tight to his legs,

Larry put him on the block and took the sack off his head. He just lay there, blinking his yellow eye, the feathers fluffed up round his neck, his wings limp. He was looking straight at Larry.

"Do it!" Larry said.

Erueti swung the axe.

The rooster let out an almighty shriek and rose off the block in a whirlwind of feathers.

The axe bit deep into the wood. Spots of blood rained down on it.

When Nanny and the others came home, Erueti was cleaning up the last of the dishes. He and Larry had put on the kettle for tea and had set out the cups with some Christmas cake.

"How was mass?" Larry asked his mother.

"If you'd been there you would have knowed," she said, still huffy with him. Then she saw the bandage on his hand. "What have you done to your finger?"

He held it up. "Ereuti — "

And Erueti said quickly, "He cut the top off with the ham knife when he was washing the dishes."

"You took the top off your finger?" Nanny said.

"Only the tip," said Larry. "It's nothing. How about a cup of tea?"

"Let me see!" said Nanny, grabbing his hand.

One of the aunties took the teapot from Larry and began pouring. "It's half past one in the morning," she grumbled. "Doesn't that rooster ever stop crowing?"

Four Winds

I have a story to tell you about a girl who lived on a beach near a small fishing village. She was not very big but she was strong and often she would go out on the boats with the fisherpeople and help them with their nets. They didn't know where she had come from. Her hair and skin were as dark as a forest at night but her eyes were the same colour as the sea when the sun shines on it. Because no one knew who her people were, she was given the name Four Winds.

The fisherpeople took care of the girl. They gave her clothing that was too small for their own children, faded jeans and T-shirts, a jacket for winter. They brought her bags of food. Some offered her a sleeping place in their homes, but Four Winds chose to remain on the beach, sharing her food with the seabirds who were her closest friends. At night she slept by her campfire, her long hair spread in the sand, while round her sat a circle of gulls and terns, oyster catchers, herons, pied stilts, gannets.

During the day, Four Winds could never go anywhere without a following of birds. Right behind her there would be bundles of feathers hopping and scuttling, and eyes like black seeds watching this side and that. Everyone in the village knew she had a feeling for birds but they didn't know how strong it was until the day the shag got caught in the net.

This day, the girl had gone on one of the fishing boats. A large snapper net was being put over the stern. The people on board were watching the net running out and splashing behind the boat, and they all saw the shag. The black and white bird popped up from nowhere, right in front of the net. In the next second it was caught in the mesh and dragged under.

"Stop! Bring up the net!" yelled Four Winds.

The fisherpeople laughed in an embarrassed way. "It's only a shag."

"Bring it up! Bring it up!" Four Winds screamed at them.

The fisherpeople had no intention of stopping the boat and pulling in the net for a mere bird. They shrugged and the net continued to splash over the stern.

Four Winds moved so fast no one could stop her. She jumped overboard into the path of the net.

There were great shouts and curses amongst the fisherpeople. They stopped the boat and hauled in the net as fast as they could, which was not very fast. First Four Winds floated to the surface and then the shag. Both were tangled in the net. Both were more dead than alive.

The shag recovered first. It swam away, beating its wings against the water until it could take flight. Four Winds did not respond so well. She started breathing again but could not move or speak or open her eyes.

The fisherpeople wrapped the girl in a blanket and turned their boat back towards the village. There, one of the fisherwomen carried Four Winds up the beach to her house. She put her in a warm bed and looked after her as though she were her own child.

For two days Four Winds lay there, neither living nor dying, and all the while, on the roof of the house, there gathered hundreds of seabirds. The corrugated iron was covered with mollymawks, oystercatchers and shearwaters, black and white shags, yellow-headed gannets, black-headed terns, and herons like thin grey ghosts. There was such a squawking and rustling, day and night, that the fisherwoman could not hear her own voice.

Gradually, Four Winds' strength came back. She opened her eyes, smiled, ate a little food. When she was well enough to sit up, the fisherwoman brushed her long hair and plaited it. It was then that the fisherwoman noticed the bumps on Four Winds' back.

"Truth in my eyes, you are growing wings!" cried the fisherwoman, but the birds on the roof were making such a noise, her words were lost. So the fisherwoman snatched Four Winds out of the bed and took her to the mirror, turning her so that she could see over her shoulder. From the edges of her shoulder blades grew two stumps like small arms, and already they were covered with soft feathers.

"Wings!" shouted the fisherwoman.

Four Winds looked and smiled and said nothing.

As Four Winds got stronger, her wings grew bigger. The fisherwoman sat down with her sewing basket and made openings at the back of the girl's shirts and jacket. Soon all the people in the village could admire the growing wings. They were now edged with strong pinions, black and white, with smaller feathers tucked smooth as silk along the upper sides. Four Winds would run along the beach, her wings beating the air in a blur of speed, and with a flock of seabirds tumbling around her.

After six months, the wings were fully grown. They were three times the length of Four Winds' arms. When they were folded at her back, they could be seen above her head, and the tips well below her knees. Like the wings of a large albatross, said the fisherpeople.

And yet Four Winds could not fly. The seabirds tried to teach her. They pecked at her wing feathers. They beat their own wings over her head. Now and then, when

Four Winds was running into a gale with her wings outspread, her feet would lift off the ground for a few seconds and then come down again. But that was all.

"There's nothing wrong with your wings," said one of the fishermen. "It's the rest of you. People shape isn't right for flying."

"Then why do I have wings?" said Four Winds.

"You'll be flying," said the fisherwoman who had looked after Four Winds. "It's the right kind of learning that's needed. Now, you take baby birds. They fly because they have to. The parents push them out of the nest."

Four Winds' eyes shone with light. She jumped up, grabbing the hands of the woman. "Thank you! Thank you!" she cried. Then she let go and ran along the beach to the high cliffs where the shags had their nests.

The fisherpeople watched as she climbed the cliff. She went up slowly, her hands and feet scraping at the rocky slope, her wings spread to help keep her balance.

"She'll be killed!" someone said.

"It's fly or die," said others.

"I reckon she knows what she's about," said the fisherwoman.

Four Winds stood at the top of the cliff. Round her, the nesting shags snaked their necks and called encouragement. Below, the sea exploded into white spray against rocks edged with kelp. In the distance, people stood on the beach, watching. Four Winds put her hands in the air like a diver. She spread her wings. Then she leaned forward.

The fisherpeople saw the small figure fall like a stone, her wings trailing behind her. Down the face of the cliff she went, twisting and turning towards the rocks. Some people screamed. Some had no breath to scream. Then, as Four Winds reached the spray of the breaking waves, her wings spread sideways. They dipped down and swept up — again, again — a slow, strong beat, and Four Winds came out of the spray, flying.

A cry went up from the fisherpeople. This was not the frantic wing-flapping they'd watched on the beach but a slow movement like a pulling of long oars. Up and down, up and down. Four Winds flew easily over the sea, her wingtips almost touching the water, then she turned her face upwards and began to climb into the sky.

The cheering from the beach was soon drowned by the clamour of gathering birds. They came from all directions, and not only seabirds. From houses and farms, from streams and trees, the landbirds came as well — clouds of sparrows and starlings, tui and kereru, blackbirds, thrushes, magpies, pukeko flapping clumsily and trailing skinny legs, wild ducks, farm geese, chaffinches, robins, bellbirds and the white cockatoo from the village store. There were so many that they blotted out the sun, and the wind from their wings made white ruffles in the water.

The people on the beach put their hands over their ears and squinted to glimpse Four Winds in the great storm of birds. One of the fishermen reckoned the only birds not flying with her were the ones in cages or plucked and dressed in freezers.

There is not much more to tell. Those who thought Four Winds would leave them now that she could fly, were wrong. The next day everything was back to normal with Four Winds sleeping on the beach, wrapped up in her wings, and the seabirds in a circle round her. The only change was that now, instead of going out on the fishing boats, she'd fly ahead of them. Sometimes she'd search out new fishing grounds. Sometimes she'd guide the boats safely through a sea mist.

The fisherpeople took care of her, the same as always, bringing her food and sometimes giving her clothes too small for their children, socks and jeans, and shirts with holes in the back for her wings.

And because there was no end to Four Winds' flying, so there is no end to her story.

The Hitchhikers

A few miles north of Dunedin they saw the hitchhikers, a man and a woman standing without coats in a mist of rain.

"Give them a ride, Mum!" yelled Max from the back of the van.

Theo called out, "No! Keep on going!"

"With a big empty van?" His mother looked at him in the rear mirror as she took her foot off the accelerator.

"We don't want any strangers," Theo said. "They look weird!"

"He ate mean flakes for breakfast," said Max.

"Squeak for yourself, brother," Theo fired back.

"Don't you two start!" their mother said, glaring in the mirror. "I've had you and your bickering. What we need is a couple of referees." She pulled up beside the hitchhikers, wound down the window and called in a voice suddenly warm with smiling, "Hop in the back with the boys."

When the hitchhikers slid open the door, they filled the van with the smell of incense, rain and wet grass. They were not young. The woman had grey in her long curly hair and the man's eyes were like quick brown fishes caught in a net of wrinkles. Theo thought they looked as though they had dressed blindfolded from a box of theatre props. The man wore a T-shirt with a bow tie painted on it and a red velvet jacket which flared at the waist over skinny black jeans. The woman had on a long orange dress with colored ribbons. Her straw hat, with more ribbons on it, was damp and like a wilted flower. Both people were beaded from head to foot with raindrops.

"I'm Chrissie," said the boys' mother. "This is Theo and that's Max."

Theo nodded but didn't speak. The couple were of his mother's generation and she was greeting them as though they had stepped out of her old photographs. She was being too cheerful, too trusting.

They threw their packs in the back of the

van and got on board, the man carrying a guitar in a padded case. "We're storytellers," he said. "You can call us anything you like."

"For starters, try Ruby and Rose," said the woman. "He's Ruby."

"Professional storytellers?" Chrissie asked.

"That's right," said Rose. "We're on our way to Oamaru. I certainly appreciate this ride."

"What kind of stories do you tell?" asked Max.

"There's only one kind of story," said Rose. "The magic kind."

Ruby laughed and settled himself in the seat in front of Max, the guitar case held between his knees. He wore black leather boots with red pointed toes and heels spattered with grass seeds. "The magic of a story depends on how far you take it. Stories have layers, you see. On the surface they're pretty ordinary but start peeling them back and you get down to the magic."

"Oamaru, Mum," Theo called.

She was in no hurry to resume the journey. She and Max were leaning towards the pair as though they were slot machines spewing out gold coins. Theo felt his back prickle with concern. What were people of that age doing hitchhiking? And why were they dressed like a couple of clowns? Maybe it was a disguise and there was a shotgun in that guitar case, and maybe the headlines in tomorrow's *Otago Daily Times* would read: *Brutal slaying of woman and two sons on lonely road.*

"What do you mean by magic?" asked Max.

"What do I mean?" The woman turned and smiled at him. "Magic changes things by extraordinary means. That's what stories do, wouldn't you say? They change our thinking, they change our way of seeing."

"Mu-um, are we going to sit here for ever?" Theo demanded.

"All right! We're going!" His mother swung round in her seat and put the van into gear. "Don't stop," she said to the couple in the rear mirror. "This is fascinating. I've never met storytellers before."

"But we are all storytellers." The woman looked surprised. "Storytelling is as much a part of the human condition as having arms and legs."

While she was talking, the man was unzipping the guitar case and Theo thought, here we go, he's making a move already. Theo put his hand behind his seat and felt for the tool kit, thinking that he should be ready with a large spanner or a jack, just in case.

The woman was saying, "As soon as you put people together they start talking about the things they've heard and seen and done and — lo and behold — you have a story."

The man looked directly at Theo, smiled as quickly as the flash of a knife and jerked down the zip of the case. He took out a guitar.

It'd be drugs, thought Theo. Drugs, for sure. Their packs were full of heroin and they avoided suspicion by hitching rides with families. Oamaru was only an hour away but maybe they were really going further and had just said Oamaru to get a lift. Maybe they were going to hijack the van and take the three of them hostage.

"Are you going to play something, Ruby?" Chrissie adjusted the rear mirror.

"Sing us a song!" Max was leaning forward, his elbows almost in the man's hair.

"What about this?" the man said, running a large brown hand up and down the stem of the guitar and trickling out chords. He began to sing:

The storyteller is a thief,
Stealing stars at night
And hammering them into dishes
For bread and butter days.

The storyteller is a magician,
Making doors that are never
Either open or shut
And windows you can put to your eyes
To see over horizons.

The storyteller is a seamstress,
Stitching the ordinary things of earth
To make wondrous garments
For long and difficult journeys.

The storyteller is a liberator,
Knocking down walls
With the thrust of a phrase
And wrenching wide open
Seed, egg, stone, brick, word,
to set truth free.

He finished with three rippling chords, looked at Theo and said, "Well?"

"It didn't rhyme," said Theo.

"Some do, some don't," shrugged the man, giving another of those quick, sharp looks which made Theo's spine creep.

"What lovely music," Chrissie said. "Do you always sing your stories?"

He replied, "I do the singing. Rose does the telling. It's Rose's turn."

"A story, is it?" Rose took off her hat and combed her long springy hair with her fingers. "How far do you want me to go with the magic?"

"As far as you can!" Max cried eagerly.

She whistled. "That's a stupendous lot of magic. Are you sure you can cope?"

"You bet!" said Max, and Chrissie laughed in the mirror.

Theo caught the sparkle in his mother's eyes and thought, This is all a game to her. She doesn't realise we're being set up. The woman starts her storytelling and while we're distracted, the man takes over. They'll probably tie us up. That's why she's got all those ribbons. They'll dump us in a flooded river and escape with the van and our gear while we quietly drown.

"What's the story to be about?" the woman said. "Give me a topic."

There was a silence.

"Look out of the window and choose something," the woman suggested.

"The police," said Theo, but no one took any notice.

To their right, the sea was soft with rain and patched with light which escaped between clouds. The tide was far out and the wet brown sand revealed half-submerged rocks, big and perfectly round.

"The Moeraki boulders," said Chrissie. "They're worth a story."

The woman craned her neck. "They are, too. What do they remind you of?"

"Big macadamia nuts," said Max.

"Cannonballs," Theo said.

The woman pointed. "There's a boulder which has broken open. It's hollow inside."

"An egg?" suggested Chrissie.

Rose nodded and smiled while Ruby quietly strummed the guitar. "And you definitely want full magic?" Rose asked. Max nodded, eagerly. Rose's voice moved to another tone, halfway between singing and speaking and her words seemed to change shape.

"On the beach at Moeraki lie a number of great round stones and for many generations, people have looked at them and wondered how they got there. Maori wisdom has one explanation and Pakeha wisdom another, but this story, fresh with the wetness of this morning's tide and rain, tells us something else.

"From the beginning, the land has lain asleep, half in the sea and half out of it, dreaming of her lover, the sky. The eyes of the sky — the sun and moon — watch over her and the breath of the sky — the wind — caresses her. So it was, until the time of World-Walker, the king of all the people, whose greed and ambition had no limits.

"World-Walker thought his kingdom far too small, so he took a small group of men and set out to wake up the land. They crossed her broad back, walked for days through her green curly hair and finally stood in the splendid cave of her ear. World-Walker stood with his men in this great hall of rock and looked up at the limestone formations which dripped and glistened in the flickering light of their torches. He called out in a loud voice, 'Wake up, oh Land! Wake up, oh mighty

Mother! Come out of your sleep and listen!'

"His voice echoed round and round the cave and came back to him from dark inner recesses. He kept on calling and finally there was a deep rumbling and shaking as the land stirred.

"World-Walker, king of all people, went on calling. 'Wake up, oh Land! Listen to your king! Why should the sea be so big and you so small? Wake! Sit up! Stand! Rise out of the ocean and claim the greatness that is rightfully yours — and mine.' There was no response, so he tried again. 'Land, you are beautiful, but so much of your beauty is hidden by the sea. If you rose out of the sea you could be twice as big, twice as beautiful.'

"No sound came from the land. The king stood there in her ear, holding up two flaming torches, while his voice echoed round and round the cave's walls. Then he had a thought. He yelled, 'Oh Land, listen! If you rise out of the sea you can get closer to your lover, Sky.'

"At that the cave began to quiver. There was a noise like the groaning of a huge hurricane, and a violent rocking that caused everyone, except World-Walker, to fall down. Stalactites broke off the ceiling and fell, shattering the stalagmites. Stones flowed down the wall in a small avalanche . . ."

"Look out!" Theo yelled. "The road's moving!"

Chrissie put on the brakes as the road rose to meet them. A flat stretch of asphalt had suddenly become a twisting snake which pushed the van to the other side and then back again.

"It's an earthquake!" Chrissie screamed, fighting for control. "I can't do anything!"

The grass and the trees at the edge of the road were blurred and the land and sky seemed to be mixed together. A clay bank split and swallowed a young pine tree.

The van slewed around so that they were facing the way they'd come. The sea was close, no longer calm but wild with dark grey waves crashing into white foam.

"The story is doing it," Rose said calmly. "Just turn around and keep going."

As she spoke, the tremors lessened and the blurred scenery came back into focus. Chrissie reversed the van in a semi-circle and then drove on, hunched over the steering wheel and white-faced. "That was the story?"

"You wanted all the magic," said Rose. Then she continued, "One of the king's men, a youth called Tarn, was fearful. He had the sense to know what the greedy king did not — that if the land rose up from sleep and really began to move, they would all be destroyed. Tarn crept out of the cave and ran through the giant's hair to the sea where he called out a message of warning to a flock of gulls. They took it to a large sperm whale who was splashing on the surface with her calf. The whale immediately went to the depths of the sea where there lived the great sea dragon.

"Now, this sea dragon held all the wisdom of the sea and some of the land and sky as well, and she knew full well the danger. 'World-Walker is a tyrant and will cause chaos if he's not stopped,' she said. So she laid a hundred beautiful eggs and set them adrift on the tide.

"Some of the eggs went to the bottom of the ocean, for dragons' eggs are extremely heavy. Some came ashore but were buried in the sand, still others — "

"Look!" yelled Max, pointing across Theo to the window.

Carried on dark waves were even darker spheres that looked like huge fishing buoys. Chrissie pulled the car up at the edge of the road and wound down her window. Max opened the sliding door and jumped out, running around the van and up a bank to see better. Rose stopped talking. The only sound, apart from the roar of the sea, was the faint trickling music of Ruby's guitar.

Max wanted Theo to get out, too, but he wouldn't. It's a trick, he thought. Once they get us all out, they'll leap into the front and drive away. He watched the dark balls as they bobbed towards the beach but at the same time he kept an eye on the couple. They were responsible for whatever was happening out there and it was all as weird as they were. Even the sea didn't appear normal. The waves were like a storm on animated film, drawings of purple and blue shapes dense with paint, exploding into white. As for the balls, they were really rocks, weren't they? Rocks couldn't float.

He thought, Maybe we've all been hypnotised.

A huge wave pushed three of the round things up the beach and then receded, leaving them on the sand. At once, one of the boulders cracked with the brittle sound of a rifle shot and something like a long, curved beak came out. Max leapt up and down on the bank, yelling.

Rose said quietly, "Tell him to get back in the van."

But neither Chrissie nor Theo said anything for they were now fully occupied watching the stone eggs which all had widening cracks. The narrow object they'd seen was not a beak but a claw and now a foot or a hand was showing, as grey as the stones of a river bed.

Then the first round egg fell apart and they saw the creature inside.

"A dinosaur!" said Theo.

"Baby sea dragons," murmured Chrissie.

"It's dangerous for Max to be out there," Rose said.

Chrissie called, "Max! Max! Come back!"

But Max had climbed further over the bank and was almost on the beach.

Theo thought the creatures looked exactly like winged dinosaurs made of living stone, as they stood there on the sand, lashing their tails back and forth, stretching their wings, and craning their necks to see about them. As they did this, they grew, unfolding like butterflies new from cocoons, until they were the size of passenger planes.

Rose said, "The magic has its own protection here, but not if he wanders away from us."

"Max? Max!" bellowed Chrissie. "Theo, go and get him."

Theo shook his head.

"Theo, did you hear me?" She grabbed the handle of her door.

"Don't go, Mum," he said. "It's a trick."

"I'll get him," said Ruby, putting down the guitar. A moment later he was leaping over the bank after Max.

This is an optical illusion, thought Theo, a mirage of some kind. When Max gets down there the dragons will disappear and spoil the trick. That's why they want him back.

The dragons were flapping their huge, scaly wings with a sound like slapping sails. One lifted a few metres off the sand and settled back.

"Hurry! Hurry!" Rose willed Ruby, her

135

voice so quiet he could not have heard.

They could see him now, his long black legs racing down the beach, his red jacket flying behind him. He was calling to Max, who had stopped and was looking back.

The dragon went up again, flew a few metres and landed not far from Ruby and Max.

"Please hurry!" breathed Rose.

Ruby grabbed Max round the waist, put him under his arm and ran back up the beach. Now all three dragons were attempting to fly and the first one was going to succeed. It was spiralling up into the sky, a great dark cloud that looked as though it were filled with thunder. With a great sweep of its wings it turned and flew towards them.

Ruby dragged Max over the bank and into the van as the dragon came up in the sky above them. The door slammed. Rose let out a sigh of relief and picked up her story.

"The eggs hatched into sea dragons, which rarely fly over the land. When they do, everything touched by their shadow turns immediately to stone."

"See there?" said Ruby.

On the bank, there was something that looked like a wide path of grey pebbles. It hadn't been there before. In it were the shapes of small shrubs and grasses, frozen into granite.

"Oh, Max!" cried Chrissie.

"I could have been made into stone!" Max squealed.

"Why didn't the van become stone?" demanded Theo. "Why didn't we?"

"This is where the story began," said Ruby. "They can't harm us here." He picked up his guitar and began to play.

Another dragon flew past. Its shadow went directly over the van and the wind from its wings rocked them. Chrissie ducked and Theo felt a cold touch of fear down his spine, but nothing happened to them. On the other side of the road, a wooden gate turned to stone and two sheep became grey monuments.

"Drive on," said Rose to Chrissie. "We're getting near the end of the story." She put her hat back on her head and continued, "The sea dragons flew along the edge of the land, which had become restless in her sleep, dreaming that her lover the sky was calling her to wake and come to him.

"Into the ear of the land flew the sea dragons and through the light of the torches, which flamed and flickered and cast great dragon-like shadows over World-Walker and his men. At once, all were turned to stone. World-Walker, instead of possessing the land, became a part of her, and today, if you ever discover the cave of the land's ear, you will see a column of stone that looks like a man with his arms raised, and around him, heaps of stone that could have been his frightened servants."

"What happened to the sea dragons?" Max asked.

"They went back to the sea," said Rose, "and everything was as before. Look down there."

Chrissie slowed down. The sea had resumed its normal colour and was flat, misty with rain. The tide was out and on the wet brown sand lay a few round boulders, some broken open as though there had been a hatching. There were no sea dragons.

Max said, "What about those sheep back there?"

"Eating grass," said Rose.

"And the plants?"

"Growing green," Rose said.

Hypnosis, thought Theo with satisfaction.

"What an experience!" said Chrissie. "Wow! That was unreal!"

"Not at all," said Ruby. "Stories are always real. It's just a different kind of reality. It doesn't have the same limits."

The rest of the journey to Oamaru passed quickly and quietly.

Rose said, "Remember I told you everyone's a storyteller? Well, some people have a special gift for getting maximum magic from a story. Ruby does. So do I. And one of you has it."

"One of us?" Max said.

Ruby turned round. "You!" he said to Theo.

Chrissie said, "Theo's got a great imagination."

Ruby smiled and his eyes were like dark fire. "Always remember that the power of your imagination is neither good nor bad. It's what you do with it that decides whether it's going to be positive or negative, creative or destructive. That is quite some responsibility."

Theo looked away from the man and didn't speak.

"Here we are," said Ruby, grabbing the

guitar and stuffing it into its case. "You can let us out at the next corner."

Theo sat quietly through the goodbyes and only when the van was moving again did he allow himself to wave towards the back window.

"Did they mean that about Theo?" Max asked Chrissie.

"I'm sure they did," she said.

Max smiled at his brother. "Tell us a story."

"I don't know any," Theo said.

"Make one up."

Theo hesitated. He was going to say something about a family who got murdered by hitchhikers but he decided against that. "You choose a topic," he said.

"Mountains," said Max. "Snow."

Theo closed his eyes and stared into blackness until Max's words formed pictures. He began, "Once there were two boys who went up a mountain. It was wintertime. Huge flakes of snow were falling and everything was very white and very cold."

"Look, you two," said Chrissie.

Theo opened his eyes. On the windscreen were flakes of snow as big as his hand.

Totara Hill

For most of the year Totara Hill wore a blanket of mist. Walking up the hill under the large, moss-covered trees was a bit like being under the sea. Lichens and wild orchids grew like coral on the tree trunks and the water that dripped down through the leaves met the water that rose in a vapour from the earth. Everything smelled of growth and decay, which is the way of all things, but on Totara Hill the smell was stronger than other places.

No one much enjoyed going there, although for the spinners and weavers of the village, frequent trips were necessary. The forest of Totara Hill was an unending source of dyestuff. People gathered berries and bark, leaves, roots, flowers, lichens that grew like hair and lichens that grew like cabbages. These things were boiled in pots with hanks of woollen yarn and then the people made clothing that contained all the colours of the forest. Travellers would come long distances to buy the garments, which were said to be more beautiful than anything made elsewhere.

It was at night that no one dared to go on Totara Hill. The villagers believed no fate was worse than being lost on Totara Hill after sunset. That's when the silver sheep came out; fabled creatures who lived in deep caves during the day and emerged to graze in the forest at night. The sheep had fleeces that looked like polished metal and there were many stories about the things that could happen to those who wore sweaters made from such fleece. Some said they could command the wealth of the world. Some said they could have the power to make themselves invisible. Others claimed they'd be able to fly. Still others said the fleece brought the gift of eternal life.

At the same time there were stories told in whispers about people who had gone up the mountain at night to catch and shear the sheep and had never been seen again.

Parents sang a warning to their children:

O, Totara Hill is dark
And Totara Hill is steep.
Strange things happen on Totara Hill
When children are asleep.

But if the children wake up
When the night is still and deep,
They will hear the singing
Of the ghostly silver sheep.

Now, it happened that a young woman spinner called Wana went to the North Island for a holiday and, to everyone's surprise, returned to the village with a husband whose name was Bram.

He was a pleasant lad, fond of talk and laughter and the comforts of life. Indeed, the only thing Bram didn't like was work and he was always looking for ways to make a lot of money with little effort. Every week he was going to win a lottery or invent something that would turn him into a millionaire, but in truth it was Wana at her spinning wheel who paid the rent and put food on the table.

When Bram first heard the stories about the silver sheep, he laughed loudly. "What a lot of superstitious nonsense!" he scoffed.

But one night he was wakened by a faint sound rising and falling on the breeze that drifted through his window. It could have been human singing; it could have been the bleating of lambs; it could have been violins or windchimes. He wasn't sure. He went out of the house and stood in the darkness while the strange music washed over him and sent shivers up his spine.

Wana came and took him by the hand. "The singing of the sheep!" she said in a fear-filled voice. "Don't listen! Come back to bed!"

The next day, Bram made Wana repeat the stories of Totara Hill. She did more. She took him to meet a weaver who had actually seen the sheep from a distance. "Like white fire in the moonlight," said the man. "Too solid for ghosts, if you ask me. Sixteen, I counted, all fully grown."

"How long have they been there?" Bram asked.

"More than a hundred years. That's right. The first settlers in the valley saw a flock of three. Then there were seven, then eleven. Now it's sixteen, so they must be breeding."

"Why is everyone scared of them?" Bram asked.

The weaver shook his head. "They're not for meddling. Those who've fancied getting some fleece have come to grief. They vanish. Or they're found dead, trampled and gored. Or else they're babbling out of their wits. Those sheep aren't of this earth, to my mind. Such things are best left well alone."

Nevertheless, Bram had already decided that he was going to spend a night on the mountain and see the sheep for himself. He dressed warmly in waterproof clothing, told Wana he was going on an overnight fishing trip, and then made a detour to Totara Hill, arriving on the lower slopes as the sun was setting. He found a safe place to hide, a shelter made by a large tree which had fallen over a hollow in the earth. It was fringed with moss and fern and damp inside but he was comfortable enough. He settled down to wait for darkness.

As time went by, he was aware that he'd heard no bird calls, no wekas squawking in the undergrowth, no bellbirds or fantails, not even a whisper of wings anywhere. The only sounds were of running water, drips and trickles in places hidden by shadow.

Whatever he was, Bram wasn't a coward. When he felt the chill edge of fear he'd push it away with thoughts of the wealth that would be his if the sheep were all that people said. Why, the richest man in the world would give half his fortune for a sweater with magic powers. Bram breathed on his cold hands and cheered himself by spending half a fortune in his imagination.

The hours passed and then the moon came up. He couldn't see it in the sky but its light washed down through the trees, frosting leaves and branches and making the shreds of mist look like snow. Everything shone. Bram said to himself, "They're probably just ordinary sheep gone bush and the silver is the trick of the moonlight. Yes, that's what it'll be."

But a few moments later he heard the music. It was much louder than the previous night, a melodic sound like the voice of a sheep captured in a windchime. It was answered by another and another and soon the tinkling cries were echoing back and forth on the upper slopes of the hill. As Bram listened they got louder, nearer. Before long there was a cascade of sound tumbling down like an avalanche, ricocheting off the tree trunks and filling the spaces between the branches.

Bram put his hands over his ears. It was as though all the bells in the world were playing at the same time. He leaned forward to peer through the ferns and his mouth fell open with amazement. The flock of sheep were coming through the trees, each a shining, metallic silver. The glistening fleeces parted along their backs and flowed down their sides, lifting, floating as they walked. They had large curled horns, eyes that glowed like red lights, and their mouths were open, breath steaming as they bleated the strange music.

Bram kept very still until they had gone by and their bleating was distant, then he came out of his hiding place. His heart was beating like a traction engine. His hands were slippery with sweat. He ran down the path to the village, and rushed into his house. "Wake up, Wana!"

"Did you get any fish?" she sleepily asked.

He laughed and danced about the room. "Fish? Who cares about fish? Tomorrow I'm learning how to shear a sheep."

When Wana realized that Bram had actually seen the sheep at close range and been unharmed, some of her fear left her. Perhaps his confident talk of a mansion by the lake persuaded her that the sheep could be shorn. At any rate, she told him everything she'd learned from the old people in the village.

"They say a great deal of care is needed. The shearing can only be done at the full moon when the sheep's strength is low. Even then they can fight like enraged bulls. But if a sack is put over the sheep's head, it will lie quiet to the shears."

"That's easy enough," said Bram.

"There's more," replied Wana. "The fleece must be spun and knitted on the mountain and until the garment is finished, there can be no sleeping or eating or drinking."

Bram laughed. "Shearing, spinning, knitting! I have a lot of learning to do. It's four weeks to the next full moon. I'd better start right now." With that he left the breakfast table and went to a neighbouring sheep farm to learn how to shear.

During the next weeks, some of the village people walked past Wana's house and saw Bram on the verandah, trying to work his hands and feet together at the spinning wheel. They smiled and said, "That young Bram has turned over a new leaf. Look at him! As industrious as you please!"

But the old people, who had seen this kind of thing before, went by in silence, shaking their heads.

What Bram lacked in natural skill, he made up for in determination. Within a fortnight he was deftly spinning a good thread and it was time for him to learn to knit. Wana sat with him while he dropped stitches and picked them up again.

"It's easy when you're used to it," she said.

"I'll never get used to it," cried Bram.

Wana shrugged. "After this you'll never need to spin or knit again."

"What do you mean?" said Bram. "There are sixteen sheep up there. Do you think I'm going to stop at one?"

When the next full moon came, Wana helped Bram pack a large sack. Into it went the spinning wheel, extra bobbins, knitting needles, a set of handshears and an old fishing net.

"Our fortune is as good as made," he said, kissing her goodbye.

One of the old people saw him striding out with the sack on his back. "Where are you going?" she asked.

"That's for me to know and you to find out," laughed Bram.

"Don't pry into matters beyond your power!" warned the old woman.

Bram paid no heed. On he went, out of the village and along the narrow track that led to Totara Hill.

He found his hollow under the log and there set up the spinning wheel with the extra bobbins and knitting needles beside it. Further down the slope, he strung the old fishing net round some trees so that it made a trap. He disguised the mesh with leaves and grasses and then went back to his shelter. With the shears in his belt and the empty sack over his knees, he waited for darkness and the rising of the moon.

It all happened as it had the month before. First came the moonlight through the trees, followed by the distant music as the sheep called to each other. Bram waited until the sound was so loud that it threatened to burst his eardrums. The sheep were very close. He leapt out of hiding, waving the sack and roaring like a lion.

The sheep froze. Their bleating stopped. They stared, their red eyes shining, their silver fleeces rising and falling rapidly with their breathing. Bram yelled again and flapped the sack. It worked. The mob broke, scattering in all directions. As he had hoped, one plunged down the slope and straight into the net.

Bram was so excited he dropped the sack. He ran to the sheep, a large ram that was caught by the horns and front legs. He flung himself upon it. But he wasn't prepared for what happened next. The sheep heaved and Bram flew backwards, striking a tree trunk that knocked the wind from his lungs. Gasping, he sat up. The animal was on its feet, still tangled in the net. It wouldn't be there for long. The mesh was being torn by slashing hooves and teeth that bit and chewed like those of a wild dog.

The sack! thought Bram. What did I do with the sack?

He found it and, holding it open, warily approached the ram. It saw him coming. It braced itself, straining against the mesh. Then it lowered its head, presenting its horns.

Bram thought, If it breaks free, I'm done for!

He manoeuvred the sack in front of the great sheep. Strands of mesh creaked and snapped. The smell of the animal was overpowering. Again it lunged towards him and the last of the net gave way, but at the same time he managed to drop the sack over its head.

The effect was instant. All fight left the sheep and it lay on the ground, grunting and panting, its silver wool rising and falling like thistledown. Bram quickly tied the sack round its neck and set to work with the shears. He was as yet a novice shearer and had expected some difficulty, but the fleece seemed almost to fly off by itself and within minutes the sheep was bare. On the ground there was a heap of wool that looked like tinsel from a Christmas tree.

For his own safety he left the sack on the sheep's head. The animal lurched into the forest, stumbling and shaking. Bram guessed that the sack would fall off some time and distance away. He gathered up the fleece, which was so light and soft he could scarcely feel it, and went back to the hollow. By the light of the moon, he began to spin. Once again, the task was amazingly easy. In spite of cramped space and limited light, the bobbins filled in record time. Over the whirr of the wheel he listened for the return of the sheep, but the forest was silent.

By dawn Bram was feeling sleepy. He kept going — spinning, plying — until the mound of fleece had disappeared and he had six bobbins of thread, which gleamed like fine silver wire. He guessed it was about midday when he began to knit. That, too, seemed effortless. The needles moved in a blur of speed and beneath them grew a marvellous sweater that shone like a coat of mail and yet was so light, it lifted with his breath. Tired and thirsty as he was, Bram could not hold his excitement. He laughed out loud. Even if it turned out that the garment had no magical powers, it was such a rare and beautiful thing that he would be able to put his own price on it.

Bram was exhausted but didn't stop knitting. He was anxious to have the sweater finished before darkness fell and the sheep came back. There had to be some truth in the stories of people found gored and trampled. Those creatures were incredibly strong.

As the sun was going down, he cast off the last stitch. There it was, knitted in one piece, the finest sweater in the world. It shone and glittered, reflecting the pink colours of the sunset. When he threw it into the air, it floated down to him gently like a leaf. He took off his waterproof coat and his red woollen shirt. This was the moment. Now he would find out if the fleece really was enchanted.

Putting his arms into the sleeves, he pulled the sweater over his head. How warm it was! How soft! It felt unlike anything he'd worn before, but nothing happened to him, no powers, no money falling out of the sky, just a tingling warmth. He was a little disappointed and remembered how tired he was.

It was time to go. He leaned forward and raised his arms to take the sweater off, but couldn't. His shoulders were heavy with fatigue, his arms stiff. He couldn't even think straight. Home, he told himself. Home,

home. He was very dizzy. He took a step forward and the weight in his shoulders brought him down to his hands and knees. He pressed his fingers into the damp earth to keep himself from falling sideways. He was afraid he was going to pass out. Maybe it was thirst. He should find water and drink.

The smell of the sweater came strongly to his nostrils, the smell of the trapped sheep. His head drooped. He looked down at the bright silver fleece which covered his arms in flowing strands. Strands? he thought stupidly. Fleece? But it was knitted, wasn't it? He lifted a hand to touch it. There was no hand there. At the end of his short silver arms were grey, ridged hooves.

Bram's cry of terror came out like the tinkling of bells.

The next day the villagers searched every part of the forest. They found the spinning wheel, the jacket and the shirt. Near them was the remains of a fishing net and, further away, an empty sack. Bram was not on Totara Hill, they said. He had disappeared.

* * *

Eventually, Wana moved away from the village. She went north and someone said she married again. Bram became another story to add to the legend of Totara Hill and the flock of sheep that was still growing, both in number and the telling. After a while the villagers couldn't even remember Bram's name. "That lazy, laughing fellow," they called him.

Everything went on as before. During the day, the spinners and weavers went up to the forest to gather dyestuffs. At night they sang the old lullaby to their children:

O, Totara Hill is dark
And Totara Hill is steep.
Strange things happen on Totara Hill
When children are asleep.

But if the children wake up
When the night is still and deep,
They will hear the singing
Of the ghostly silver sheep.

Fire Mist

Earth and Sky had been married for many ages and had parented thousands of children, when Sky's brother, Sun, fell in love with Earth's sister, Rain. They wanted to marry. Both Earth and Sky laughed at the idea.

"You can never live together," they said. "Sun, she will put out your fire. Rain, he will dry you up. What can you be thinking of?"

Sun and Rain knew of the dangers but they went ahead and married. The partnership was not an easy one and every time they were together there were thunderstorms, but they continued to love each other and in time they had a beautiful daughter whom they called Fire Mist. The child had skin as cool as a river stone but her eyes glowed like orange flame and her hair, which she wore tied up on her head, carried in it all the light and fire of Sun and every cool colour of Rain.

Sun and Rain kept their daughter hidden in a valley by a lake. As the girl grew to be a woman, both parents were afraid of losing her to some young man. They kept a watchful eye on their daughter's movements but one day the inevitable happened.

There was a young man called He-who-sings, who had a voice that could charm anything on Earth. When he sang, trees shivered and dropped leaves, streams stopped running to listen, flowers unwrapped themselves from their buds. At the sound of his voice, unborn babies smiled in their mothers' wombs and dreamed of light. Some even said that when He-who-sings did his song for the dying, Death kicked up his heels and danced away over the horizon, never to return. But that may not have been true.

When He-who-sings came to the valley by the lake, he was surprised at the silence about him. Mist hung like grey cloaks over the trees and everything smelled of water, yet there was no sound of dripping or splashing, no noise at all. Afraid that it might be a place of dark enchantment, He-who-sings raised his head and sang a blessing to sweeten the air.

Fire Mist had slipped out of the cave she shared with her mother, and was sitting on a rock by the lake tying up her hair. She heard a sound which made her heart open up like a flower and the blood in her veins hum like a swarm of summer bees. Where could such sweetness come from?

She ran down the valley, following the song, and came upon a young man singing with his face turned to the sky. When he saw her he stopped and stared.

Fire Mist, who had never seen anything like him before, said, "What kind of creature are you?"

The young man went on staring at her and could find no words.

"What are you? What is that sound you make?" Fire Mist asked.

"I am your cousin, He-who-sings. You must be Fire Mist. I've heard about you. Everyone says you're the most beautiful woman who has ever lived."

Fire Mist did not altogether understand what he was saying but his face shone with a look that made her eager to know him. They stood there near the lake and talked until Fire Mist heard her mother calling.

"I will be back this evening," said He-who-sings. "Listen for my song and come to me."

When Fire Mist returned, Rain immediately noticed a difference in her. The young woman was breathing quickly and the flames in her eyes danced so brightly that they lit the cave.

"Have you been talking to someone?" Rain demanded.

Fire Mist was afraid. "No, Mother," she said, lowering her eyes.

"What were you doing down by the lake?"

"I was simply putting up my hair, Mother," Fire Mist said.

Rain was not convinced. That night she stayed awake to watch her daughter, who was showing those signs of love that Rain knew so well. Sure enough, when the night was deep and dark, a soft, wondrous singing came floating into the cave. As magical as the sound was, Rain knew two things: the singer was a young man and he was in love.

Fire Mist got up from her sleeping mat and hurried out of the cave. Down the valley she went, running in the darkness with sure, eager steps. Further back, Rain followed.

In the clearing by the lake stood a young man, singing of love. Although the night was black, the trees and water near him shone as though there were a full moon. Fire Mist ran to him. The singing stopped and they held each other. Rain watched from the shadows and knew that the time she dreaded had come.

The next morning, while Fire Mist slept, Rain heaped large stones in front of the cave and set them with a spell. Then she called through a small gap to waken her daughter and tell her why she was being kept a prisoner. Fire Mist wept and pleaded but Rain would not listen. She went off to tell Sun about the young man.

He-who-sings was in his village when a violent storm erupted out of a fine day. Clouds boiled up from nowhere, lightning slashed the sky, and thunder exploded over the gardens, sending everyone rushing to their houses for shelter. He-who-sings guessed what had happened. In spite of the heavy rain, he ran to the lake and up through the valley, looking for his beloved. The rain came down like an angry waterfall, threatening to wash off his skin. He could barely see. But he kept searching until he found the cave with the entrance blocked by piles of rock. His heart told him that this was the place. He saw a small gap in the stones and called to Fire Mist. She answered at once and told him what had happened.

"I shall tear down these stones and take you to my village," he said.

"You cannot," said Fire Mist. "My mother has placed a spell on them. No one can move them."

He-who-sings tried to shift a small rock but couldn't. He put all his weight against it. It was like trying to move a mountain.

"I will have to stay here forever," said Fire Mist.

He-who-sings laughed. "This is a game

that two can play. Stand back. I know how to release you."

He-who-sings took a deep breath, opened his mouth, and sang a powerful song about a love that could move the earth. His mother Earth heard it, sighed, and shook a little to release the spell on the stones. They tumbled out of the mouth of the cave. In the next instant, Fire Mist and He-who-sings were in each other's arms.

Far away, Rain knew what was happening. She felt the spell she had made snap inside her like a twig, and she stopped talking to Sun and listened. She said, "They're together. He has sung down the stones."

"His voice has much power," said Sun.

"That is because my sister Earth helps him," said Rain. "But your brother Sky doesn't take sides in family affairs. If you brought Fire Mist up here to live with you, then neither Earth nor that singing son of hers would be able to reach her."

"That is very wise," said Sun. "We shall build her a house of cloud and she can stay here where we can both keep an eye on her."

When Fire Mist and He-who-sings reached the village, the storm was over. They were running hand-in-hand to He-who-sing's house when a white cloud suddenly came down from the sky. It wrapped itself round Fire Mist, dragging her away from her lover's hand, and took her up into the air. It hung below the Sun like a little white house, with Fire Mist inside it.

He-who-sings stared up at the cloud. He sang loudly of grief and longing but his voice had no power beyond the earth and although Fire Mist heard him, she could do nothing. Her father Sun watched her from above, her mother Rain watched her from below. There was no way she could escape.

But He-who-sings would not give up. Hour after hour, he sat beneath the cloud house singing, while Fire Mist, helpless, listened to his love.

Two days passed, and it was time for Rain to meet Sun again. As always, when they met the air became hot and humid and dark thunderclouds gathered, completely hiding the little white cloud, which hung like a bird cage with Fire Mist inside it. The young woman listened to the deep rumbling of her parents' conversation while further away, like a silver thread, came the sound of He-who-sing's voice.

Fire Mist knew that Sun and Rain would be busy all day. This was her chance to be with the man she loved.

Fire Mist pulled the ties from her long, long, wondrous hair and let it fall in two billowing strands from the cloud house. Down, down it went, shimmering with every imaginable colour, down until it touched the ground at the feet of He-who-sings. He reached for the strands, which were as light as air and as strong as love, and he began to climb.

While Sun and Rain rumbled and grumbled, laughed and wept, flashed with dancing and crashed with thunder, He-who-sings climbed into the white cloud house and stayed all day with his beloved Fire Mist.

After that, whenever Sun and Rain spent time together, so did Fire Mist and He-who-sings. And, strange as it may sound, Sun and Rain never found out.

The people in the village knew, however. Whenever they could not find He-who-sings, they would look into the clouds, and if they saw a rainbow they would nod and say, "So that is where he is."

Ghost Town

They pushed their bikes up the last part of the hill, not because it was too steep but because the track was so overgrown that dockweed and dead thistles were weaving themselves through their wheels.

"No one's been here for months," said Robyn, freeing her front spokes of dried grasses.

"Years, probably," said Carl, looking back down the slope. "You wouldn't get this far in a four-wheel-drive, and there aren't many mad enough to bike thirty k's on a road to nowhere."

"Nowhere now," said Robyn, "but I'll bet it was busy in its time." Her foot turned on something in the weeds. She reached down and pulled up a brown glass beer bottle with the label DB BITTER. "There's an antique for your collection."

He sighed. "Find a full one, will you? I'm as dry as one of your jokes."

The pine trees came up first, rising darkly over the hill, their twisted arms raised to take the weight of the sky. Then came a solitary chimney of brick and mortar, growing out of the weeds like a memorial. It wasn't until they came up on the plateau that they saw the house and, further on, some rusting iron sheds.

They stopped to get a couple of cans of lemonade from one of the packs. Carl dragged up his T-shirt to wipe the sweat off his face. "What did that guy at the motor camp say?"

"Plenty. He talked for hours."

"I mean about the size of this place."

"About twenty houses and a two-roomed school, but it's all gone now. Buildings removed or burned." She gulped the lemonade and wiped her mouth with the back of her hand. "Apparently, they took the coal down the hill in wagons, right down to the coast where it was shipped out. He reckons there's still a huge coal seam in there but you'd never get to it. Far too unstable, he said. The last big cave-in was in 1944."

Carl whistled. "Half a century ago! You'd

think with modern mining techniques they'd reopen it."

"Maybe no one wanted to, what with three men buried in there." Her voice dropped almost to a whisper. "Imagine taking in machinery and digging up three skeletons."

He laughed. "Or chucking someone's bones on the fire."

"Carl, that's gross!"

"It's the origin of the word bonfire. Bone fire. Didn't you know?" He drained the aluminium can, crushed it and pushed it back in the pack. "Ah well, this isn't making our fortune. Where do we look?"

"Campsite first, treasure later," she said. "What about that old house?"

"Probably full of rats."

"Not if it's been deserted for years. It's going to be a cold night and I'd rather be in a house than a tent. It's got a chimney. We might even get a fire going."

"Romantic," said Carl. "Rats in our sleeping bags, wetas in our clothes and possum poo sandwiches."

"Better than frostbite."

"Yeah, yeah, maybe. Let's see if we can get in."

The house was a small cottage of un-painted wood, rough with cracks and lichen and wearing a roof of rusted iron. The ve-randah had gone, leaving a number of foun-dation posts sticking up through the grass like weathered tree stumps. There were boards nailed over the windows and doors.

As they walked round it, Robyn found the remains of a garden, a lemon tree with more wood than leaves, and a patch of wild mint, the fragrance of which came up thick with childhood memories of roast lamb. Had children played here? she wondered. And the miners who were killed — had any of them belonged to this house?

They made a wide path about a spread-ing rose bush covered with orange hips, and came round again to the front. Carl un-strapped the spade from his bike and used it as a lever to prise off the planks that cov-ered the door. With the spade handle, he pushed in one of the door panels, reached in and pulled back the lock.

The door opened directly into the main room, which was quite dark. Light filtered in through gaps in the boards on the win-dows, and slanted across the room in narrow bars thick with dust. It was a while before they could see anything else. The walls were hung with ragged scrim, cobwebs and a faded picture from an old calendar. The floor was covered with green painted lino and dust. There was no furniture, only a small, plain fireplace, which appeared to be in working order.

To the side were two small rooms, and out the back, the remains of a kitchen. Carl poked about but there was nothing to be salvaged. Even the cupboard doors and taps had been taken. In one of the small rooms stood a set of rusty bunks. They took one look at the broken wires and decided they'd spread their sleeping bags on the floor in front of the fire.

They wheeled in their bikes. Carl thought he might fossick a bit before dark.

"Take the torch and look under the house," Robyn suggested.

He shook his head. "That's the first place people look. It'll all have been picked clean as a whistle. No, the idea is to poke around for a midden. Some place where the ground has subsided — that's often a sign. Everything got buried in those days, medals and marbles, bottles and jars, wrought-iron bed ends, button hooks, coal miners . . ." He grinned. "Catch you later."

Robyn gathered a bunch of pine twigs and used them to sweep the floor. She spread out the tent, unrolled their sleeping bags on it, unpacked the food and filled the fire grate with pine needles and some dry cones. She took the matches out of her pack and was about to light the fire when she realised that the chimney was stuffed with straw. Birds' nests! The room would fill up with smoke. The way to deal with that problem was to get up on the roof and shove some burning paper down the chimney — burn them out from the top. She tucked the matches and some paper in her pockets and went out to look for Carl.

She bet herself that he'd find something valuable. He always did. He had a nose like a metal detector, his father said, and Robyn had to agree.

Until she'd met Carl, she hadn't thought much of history. Her school experience had left her with the conviction that history couldn't be taken seriously. With the human appetite for propaganda, exaggeration, manipulation and outright lying, who in their right mind would trust a history text to be true?

Then she got a boyfriend who worked with his father in an antique and curio shop and she realised history wasn't books, it was people. You could actually touch lives long gone by placing your fingertips over theirs on the objects they'd once possessed — the key of an 18th century clock, an ostrich feather from an Edwardian hat, a hair brush, a gold locket.

She remembered how she'd felt when Carl had given her an old Roman coin with a hole in it. He'd said that the hole was for carrying it on a string round the waist or neck. As she'd held the coin between her thumb and forefinger, pressing flesh together through the hole, she'd been overwhelmed by the weight of the lives of everyone who had handled the coin down the ages. She wasn't looking at a book full of words and dates. This was a long, living line like an umbilical cord which went far back out of sight to something she knew and didn't know, which was a part of her.

That's what history was — a cord. People got threaded on it and death didn't remove them.

Robyn left the house and walked towards the only other buildings, the two iron sheds that were tucked against the hill on the other side. That's where the old mine was. And this, she thought, looking round at the space filled with grass and lupin, this must have been the road to the mine, with tracks down the middle for the coal trucks. No trace of it now.

Just suppose, she thought, that people left an invisible layer on everything they touched. And suppose someone invented a camera that could take a picture of that layer, showing it as bright red. Think of the footprints on this road. There'd be no wilderness of weeds but a bright red carpet, deep as a mattress, laid down by miners and their wives, grandparents, children, lovers, travelling merchants and bankers, school teachers, doctors and drunkards.

She stopped and looked behind her. She had created a phantom crowd, which she half expected to see silently following her.

There was nothing but the sun shining low like a burning cross in the pines. In spite of it, the air was very cold. She hugged herself and went on, past some bedraggled fence posts, past an old water tank lying on its side, and on to the mine entrance.

Actually, there was no entrance, for it had been covered with sheets of iron and the only indication of an opening was the trickle of coal dust that had spilled out under the barrier. There were words of warning printed large on the iron in dribbling red paint. KEEP OUT! DANGER! DO NOT ENTER! Above, the hill looked harmless enough — layers of rock patched with grasses and small shrubs — but she was thinking once more of the three miners and their moment of terror as the hill collapsed on them. Again, her imagination took over. Out there in the open, she felt a mountain of rock coming down on her, crushing out her breath. Her ears filled up with shouts of alarm and weeping.

She shook her head roughly. The sounds, the feeling of panic, left her. She turned away to look in the old iron sheds.

A few minutes later, she found Carl between the pines and the house. He had cleared an area of grass and was digging. To one side lay a green soda bottle and two small blue castor oil containers.

She said, "I looked in the old shed. Nothing there."

"So did I," he said. "It's been well stripped. But I think I'm on to something here. It's a midden, all right. I found a couple of old kerosene tins and some barbed wire in the grass. People tend to put their rubbish in one place, so I figured there might be something underneath. There you are!" A lump of dirt had fallen open to reveal a Blue Willow cup, but when he picked it up, they saw that part of it was missing. He threw it into the grass. "You wouldn't say this was Royal Doulton country but sometimes you get lucky. I once dug up a rotten old leather bag full of surgical instruments and glass-stoppered bottles. They were in mint condition. Wouldn't mind betting there are some interesting bits and pieces in that old mine. Tools, maybe. Rope, pulleys, picks — "

"You're not going in there!"

"Wouldn't hurt to take a look."

"It's not safe! Anyway, it's all sealed up."

"So was the house." He stood up, wiping the earth off the spade. "I wouldn't go right in the mine. I'm not that dumb. I'd just stand at the entrance and have a look. Where did we put the torch?"

"Carl, you can't do it now."

"Why not?"

"You just can't!" She indicated the house. "I need you to hoist me up on the roof."

"The roof? What for?"

"Chimney's full of birds' nests. I have to burn them out before we can light the fire."

"I'll fix that later. Come on. Five minutes is all it'll take."

"Have a look tomorrow. Carl, I want to get that fire alight. It's getting dark — "

"And cold," he said. "And there's a singular lack of firewood round here, have you noticed?"

"I've got some pine cones."

"Indeed, my lady!" He picked up one of the rusted kerosene tins. "And why use pine cones when there might be a fine lot of coal for the carrying?"

"Please, Carl! Leave it!"

He grinned. "If you don't want to come, that's okay by me. I won't be long."

She hesitated. "All right, I'll go — as

long as we don't go into the mine. Agreed? Just stand outside with the torch?"

"Yes, ma'am," he said. "Certainly, ma'am."

Carl carried the spade and kerosene tin. Robyn held the torch. The sky had the faded blue look of early evening and the grass was now quite wet with dew. Above their heads, swarms of insects were on the move.

Carl set to work with the spade on the sealed entrance to the mine. The timbers that shored up the opening were rotten and the nails pulled out easily enough, but the noise of it filled the evening, metal shrieking against metal as sheets of iron came loose and then fell like thunderclaps. It wasn't long before he could see in. He became very excited. "There are rails in here, and a coal wagon! It's wooden. Got fantastic wheels!" He worked faster. "We've struck oil, Robyn!"

Another sheet of iron, with DO NOT painted on it, came down. Carl kicked it away and swung aside the remaining sheet which bore the message ENTER! Robyn switched on the torch and came closer. The coal truck was sitting just inside the tunnel, on iron rails. When she shone the torch beyond it, she saw that the rails disappeared down the throat of the mine. Lumps of loose coal lay everywhere.

"Carl, let's fill the tin and go."

He took the torch from her and went inside the entrance to examine the wagon. "It's still got some coal in it, you know that? I can get those wheels off, dead easy."

"Let's go, Carl. Please!" The cold, stale breath of the mine brought back her feelings of panic, and her voice had grown shrill.

"Yeah, yeah, no worries." He was waving the torch about, looking further in. The blade of light sliced up and down the dark uneven walls and timbers. Then he stopped. "You beauty!" he exclaimed. "Robyn, look at that!"

"Where?"

"Over there — hanging on a spike."

In the circle of yellow light she saw a plank against the rock and, hanging from it, a small cylinder. "What is it?"

"A Davey miner's lamp. Scarce as hen's teeth these days."

"Leave it there, Carl!"

"I won't be a jiff."

As the torch light shifted, the object on the wall seemed to swing.

"Carl!"

But he was already moving into the mine to get it. With the torchlight in front of him, all Robyn could see was part of his silhouette. His footsteps were loud in the coal dust. There were other sounds, too, welling up in her head, deep rumblings, shouts and cries, weeping so diluted by the years that it was as thin as gauze curtains blowing back and forth in the wind. She couldn't control her fear. "Carl! Come back!"

Now the light shone fully on the lamp and he was reaching for it. She saw his left arm raised, saw his face split with a grin. "A genuine Davey! Choice condition, not a — *aaaagh!*"

The torch fell. In the darkness his shriek went on and on.

"Carl!"

"I'm caught!" His voice was urgent with pain. "A trap!"

"What kind of trap?" She moved into the entrance, not knowing what to do. She heard him struggling and grunting, but all she could see was a small half-moon of light on the ground, where the torch had fallen.

The voices of her imagination came up like a discordant choir and she wanted to turn and run. "Carl? Carl? Say something!"

"Get the torch!" he yelled.

She froze. She couldn't go in there. She couldn't. Her legs wouldn't move.

"The torch! Hurry!"

She crouched low, her hands out in front of her, and took a couple of steps towards the yellow spot of light. Her feet slid on the coal dust and she put her hands down, felt a metal rail.

Carl screamed. "The bloody thing's alive!"

On hands and knees now, she scrambled for the light and grabbed the body of the torch. Still kneeling, she swung it round.

Carl was less than a metre away in the same place she'd last seen him. The lamp was above his head to the left and he was leaning away from it, his body angled out from the wall. But his lower left arm was against the wall and there was something over his wrist, a big handcuff, dark, moving.

She stood up, bringing the torch closer. It wasn't a handcuff. It was a hand! A hand on the wall was holding Carl's wrist in a locked grip.

Carl was grunting with pain and terror. He tried to prise open the fingers. "It — it's not real. Hard as stone. It's moving!"

There was no hole in the wall behind the hand. It was part of the rock and yet it was a man's hand, all right. The knuckles were thick, the fingertips splayed and the nails cracked. It was deeply ingrained with coal dust.

"Let go!" Carl yelled, beating it with his right fist.

Whatever the hand was made of, it had changed. It was fading, losing substance somehow. The wall and Carl's wrist were showing through it like a photograph double-exposed.

"Hit it with the torch!" Carl cried at Robyn.

"It's going!" She pushed the light closer. "It's disappearing!"

The hand was now only an outline.

"No it isn't! Hit it!"

It faded completely. The light shone on Carl's arm and the solid black wall behind it. Nothing else was there.

Then, as Robyn looked, the flesh on Carl's wrist moved and deep patches of red, streaked like raw meat, spread over his skin. He screamed with pain.

"There's nothing to hit!" cried Robyn.

"Give it to me!" He snatched the torch from her, swung it over his head and brought it down on his wrist. It struck like a clang. Immediately Carl's body was jerked sideways and he shrieked again as his left arm was slammed three times against the wall. The torch fell on the ground.

Robyn picked it up and shone it on him. The outline of the hand was there again, but it quickly faded. It seemed to be sensitive to light.

Carl's arm was held against the wall and on the dark red of his bruises there appeared four deep white marks. Slowly the arm began to twist.

"It's breaking my arm!" Carl screamed.

Robyn reached out to touch his wrist. Her fingers stopped on something cold and hard — and moving. In fear, she snatched her hand back and held it against her chest. Something rattled in her jacket pocket and she remembered the matches. Fire! she thought.

She put the torch under her arm and with shaking hands, took out three matches from the box. She held them together and struck them all at once. As the flames leaped up, she thrust them towards Carl's wrist.

The invisible hand ignited. Its outline reappeared as yellow and blue flame raced over it, burning like a halo round Carl's wrist. At the same time, the whispering voices grew louder. Sounds rushed through the mine like a wind and Robyn was aware of a great groaning like the noise of rocks falling away from themselves. The flames grew larger, brighter than the torch. Carl's arm dropped from under them and he fell back towards her.

The hand was writhing, invisible still, but traced by the pattern of fire. It moved along the wall and the fingers flexed. Then it seemed to retreat into the rock. For a couple of seconds five blue flames flickered on the wall, then went out. The noises disappeared with it and now there was only the yellow light of the torch and the sound of their sobbing.

They stumbled into the open where insects still rose and fell and an evening star hung in a sky tinged with sunset. They were both crying. Carl couldn't move his fingers without sickening pain and they knew there was some bone broken. Robyn wanted to make a sling but he wouldn't stop for it, not even at the house.

Robyn shoved tent, food and sleeping bags into the packs. Carl held his left arm against his chest under his parka, and carried the torch in his right hand. Robyn pushed both bikes.

The spade was still at the mine. Neither of them mentioned it. They didn't even pause for the bottles Carl had found. They struggled on down the hill, fighting waist-high weeds in the dark. Carl was moaning. Every footfall hurt him. He kept saying, "What was it? What was it?"

Robyn couldn't answer. Her teeth were chattering and her shoulders shaking so much that she could scarcely steer the bikes.

It wasn't the hand she was seeing. In her mind, fixed like a photo in a frame, was an image of Roman coins threaded on a string which had no beginning and no end.

Biographical Notes
on the Author

— *Born in Levin on 7 August 1936*

— *Spends about three months every year working in other countries, talking in schools, lecturing, running writing workshops*

— *Special interests include writing for early reading, for children with reading difficulties and for children who have English as a second language*

— *Hobbies are spinning and weaving, painting, boating, fishing and reading*

— *Awarded Commemoration Medal for services to New Zealand 1990; OBE for services to children's literature 1992; Margaret Mahy Lecture award, Woman's Suffrage Centennial Medal, Hon. D.Litt. Massey University, 1993*

— *Received Children's Book of the Year Award 1982; AIM Book of the Year Award 1992*

— *Married to Terry Coles, with two sons and two daughters, and nine grandchildren*

— *Lives in Kenepuru near Picton*

Joy Cowley Comments

What were my early interests? I enjoyed making things, especially with wood. Used to spend all my pocket money on nails. Was slow to become a fluent reader but when I discovered the magic of storybooks I couldn't get enough of them. At the age of eleven I had an accident on my bike — ran into a parked van because I was reading a book on the handlebars. Very embarrassing. I used to tell my younger sister stories every night, and also wrote stories for the children's page of the newspaper *The Southern Cross*.

I began writing for early reading when my son Edward was having much the same problems with reading as I'd had. I'd like to write reading texts for older children and adults who need to develop reading skills.

Reading should be "magic." Humor is valuable (children can't be tense when they're laughing) and also rhyme, rhythm, alliteration, etc. The two crimes in early reading are giving children books which are dull, and books which are difficult.

From *Beneath Southern Skies: New Zealand Children's Book Authors & Illustrators* by Tom Fitzgibbon and Barbara Spiers, Ashton Scholastic 1993.